A Ferry Long Way to Go
The Charmed Inn Mysteries 3
Misty Simon

PRAISE FOR MISTY SIMON:

"Cozy fans will be charmed."
-Publishers Weekly
"A mystery like no other I have read."
-Lisa K's Reviews Blog
"You'll be cheering as the clues pile up in this creative cozy mystery."
-Lynn Cahoon, *New York Times* bestselling author
"A down-to-earth heroine."
-Kirkus Reviews
"An amusing new series with an engaging, spirited sleuth."
-Library Journal
"A cast of entertaining characters."
-Kings River Life Magazine
"Simon has you laughing out loud."
-Cozy Mystery Book Reviews

GET THE WHOLE SERIES NOW!

Chapter 1

"Roxy, I need that recipe! I cannot possibly make anything else for this brunch. You have to understand that." Glennis was yet again in a tizzy, and I was going to have to figure out how to deal with her before we both lost our cool.

As per usual, when dealing with my wonderfully talented, but fabulously irritating, head chef at my inn, I did everything I could to not roll my eyes. She gave me more headaches than I wanted to count, but I didn't want to get rid of her, because she was awesome, and some headaches could be worth it.

This one I was struggling with, though. I had an entire inn of people who already had their cars packed and were only waiting for one last brunch before they'd head out, and I could start my much-anticipated vacation. Maybe if I could be understanding and encourage her to just make something else, it would all be better.

It wouldn't happen, but I could always hope. That was me, Roxy Gleason, eternally hopeful, even if I got smacked with reality several times a week when I walked into this kitchen.

On any other day, we would have had an audience in here, with the other two women who also staffed the kitchen. But they were both out in the dining room next door, setting up the tables, chatting amicably, and smiling at each other. Lucky them. They got to have fun, whereas I was in here with a woman who I was pretty sure was a half-second away from shooting fire out of her eyes.

"I don't know what to tell you, Glennis. I'm sorry. Can't you look it up on the internet? There has to be something out there that is close. You've made the thing a thousand times here, how do you not have it memorized by now?"

Her eyes narrowed to slits and her hands clenched into fists. Oops, obviously that was the wrong thing to say.

"This is no joke, and it's not just something you randomly pull off the internet. You have absolutely no respect for anything I do or how I do it. That's unacceptable, and I'll be talking to your grandfather about that right now." She whipped off her apron and threw it on the prep counter to her left.

I wasn't sure what was going on with her to make her so angry, but she'd been off kilter this whole week. Just now, I realized I should have asked sooner if everything was okay. I had been so wrapped up in getting things ready for everyone to leave on their much-needed and well-deserved vacations that I hadn't been paying enough attention to what was happening in the now.

I very calmly placed myself in front of the door out to the hallway. She could, of course, turn around and take the back door out of the kitchen that led to the backyard. But before she walked out the door to talk to my grandfather, who no longer owned this inn, because I did, then we were going to pause for her to hear what I had to say, what I should have said before.

"Move," she growled in a voice that was low and filled with shades of rage.

"I'm not moving, Glennis, until you hear me out, please. I'm sorry you don't think I take you or your work seriously, because I promise you I do. I think you're amazing and value you, both as a person and as an amazing cook. I'm sorry, too, that I did not understand how important the recipe is, and I apologize for coming off flip about it. I'll go out and look for the recipe to see if maybe it got misplaced."

She harrumphed, but her shoulders sank from framing her ears to half-mast.

"As far as I know, no one has been in the kitchen, but the three of you in the last twelve hours. Well, maybe Mena, too," I said, gesturing at the sink where it looked like she probably left her ice cream bowl. "Did you lock the door behind you when you left last night?"

She nodded. Maybe she didn't trust herself to say anything nice right now, and so was choosing not to say anything at all. I was on board with that.

"Did you see the recipe last night before you left?" Her shoulders rose, and I was quick to explain. "I'm not saying you should have, or that you'd need to. I just want to make sure I know the last time it was seen, so I can know where to look or who to ask. Please, work with me here."

Those shoulders went all the way down to their normal position. She shook out her head and her torso and blew out a breath. "I did see it last night. I put it out on the counter to use it this morning."

"Okay, so it was out on the counter, and the door had been locked. But that doesn't mean someone with a key couldn't have opened the door. And maybe, when they did come in, they brought a breeze in that they didn't feel. Or they created the breeze when they swished open the refrigerator door, or as they walked by. The recipe could have flown off the counter and floated onto the floor?"

"I looked."

"I'm sure you did. But could it have maybe been stepped on and stuck to someone's shoe? Or maybe it got kicked out of the way. It could be in the hallway. It could be in the lobby."

That seemed to give her pause, and that pause was what I'd been looking for. "Why don't you prepare everything else you need, set the oven, if you know about what the temp is, and I'll go out and search around like a dog looking for treats. I promise I'll come back as soon as I find it. I'm sure that will be soon." Especially if I used my dubious talent of bibliomancy to ask for where this recipe could be. Sometimes, when I posed a question to a book and then flipped to a random page, I was graced with an answer.

It was called a "talent" in my family, but felt dubious sometimes, especially when other people in my line could do much cooler things. But lately I'd grown to appreciate it more because it had started working with fireworks and clear information. I could hope for that this time, too. Of course, sometimes it told me to grab an umbrella when I asked if the printer needed toner, so there was no guarantee.

Glennis gave me one more slitty-eyed look before nodding her head again. Finally, she grabbed her apron and looked at the floor as she put it back on. She got a glass out of the cabinet above her head, and while she didn't exactly slam it onto the counter, it did clink a little louder than it needed to.

"I'll be back. Do you want Taylor and Clara to come back in and help, or should they continue to work in the dining room?" I wish I knew what was going on with her. This couldn't all be about a single recipe, no matter how much she loved it. Now was not the time to ask, though. Maybe once I found it, and the guests from this week were gone, we could sit down and have a real talk.

However, if there was anything I'd learned since taking over the inn from my grandfather, who I affectionately called Poobah, it was that you often had to kowtow to any number of people, both employees and guests, if you wanted to get what you were looking for.

And if skulking around the hotel while looking for a recipe card from the 1900s was in the cards today, then those were the ones I was going to play.

I left Glennis humming to herself in the kitchen. It sounded more like a dirge than a put-the-pep-in-your-step song, but I was not going to call her out on her music choice. I apparently had a recipe card to find and no freaking idea where it might have wandered off to.

Then again, there was every possibility that instead of someone else taking the recipe, *something else* might have, like our resident ghost. But Earl hadn't been up here in months, and when he did want something, he tended to call me on the phone hidden beneath the stairs leading to the foyer.

Which was where I was headed right now. I might as well start with the closest area and work out from there. Maybe if I placed a call to him, he would have seen something to help me find this recipe card.

I wished my boyfriend, Dean, were here to help because he always seemed able to find the unfindable. But it was peak ferry season on the river down the street, and so he was on shift, sometimes double shifts right now. Soon enough, though, we'd be on that vacation I couldn't wait for. Once the huge family that was staying here for their family reunion left, and we took a few days to get everything back where it belonged, everyone was leaving on vacation. Except for me and Dean. We had agreed that a staycation was much more our speed, and we planned to play house in this huge monstrosity I called home. Without staff, without family onsite, without guests. I couldn't wait. His brother Caper and Caper's two kids, who I adored, would still be in the small cottage out back that they were making into a home, but that was fine with us.

First, though, I had to find a recipe. After that, I would then have to deal with checking everyone out, following the meal that

Glennis was so worried about being perfect that she couldn't just make one of her other fabulous quiches and call it done. I kept my gaze on the ground as I made my way out of the kitchen and turned left toward the lobby. Taking a quick glance into the dining room on my way past, I heard Clara and Taylor discussing how fun the last week was. We'd hosted the family reunion, and other than a couple of hiccups, it really had been a lot of fun.

As the only family here, they'd filled every room with their laughter and telling stories to each other. They'd relaxed here, playing games in the billiard room, listening to music in the sitting room, and having tea and coffee in the dining room. The one woman, Penny Deitz, who'd paid for the whole thing, was a retired librarian, so she'd been in my two-story library many times, her fingers wandering over book spine after book spine, oohing and ahhing with her grandchildren over our extensive inventory.

When she booked the inn, she had specifically asked us not to set up any planned activities like game nights or picnics or even breakfast, which were all usually included in the price of the stay. She'd wanted things to happen organically, not on a timed schedule. The only meal Penny had requested was this last morning's brunch before they left. Other than that, they had just wanted to go out to local restaurants for all meals and desserts. Or they had bought a couple of catered picnics through the local grocer.

Glennis had been a little irritated that they wouldn't let her make those lunches or set up prime dinners, but Penny had been adamant. We did have snacks in the kitchen, and a few times this week the kids had come knocking on the door or dinging the bell at the front desk for Aunt Hellen to get them some cream puffs Glennis just happened to have on hand. She'd been happy to provide them, of course.

But this brunch was her one hurrah when it came to this crowd, and I understood her wanting to make it a big to-do. I just wish she would unbend a little. She was going on vacation next week, too, and had only worked part-time this week. For their part, both Clara and Taylor had decided to work alternate days from each other until today and had enjoyed some away time, which benefited all of us since I had little for them to work on if the families in the inn weren't actually in the inn. We'd had one other guest on the third floor, but he had barely emerged from his room and had left yesterday.

But my ladies were here today, darting around in the dining room and getting things ready for this brunch that I hoped would go off without a hitch. Or if the hitch had to be around, maybe it could be the size of one on the back of a compact car instead of the hitch that Dean used to pull the ferry out of the river in the off-season.

I was so lost in my own thoughts and looking at the floor, thinking we should probably have someone come in and clean these carpets, that I didn't hear the low-level arguing going on in the lobby until I was almost on top of the family.

"I don't understand why we have to do it this way. There's nothing wrong with deciding on a different course and then taking it. We outnumber her, Sally."

Using my peripheral vision only, I could see Sally had pressed her lips together to the point that they wrinkled in her already lined face, and then she darted a glance over my way before looking back at her husband.

If I could have ducked out of the room, I would have. Or even just kept moving through as if I had heard nothing and seen nothing. Sometimes that was an innkeeper's best defense, as long as it didn't involve any damage to my property.

But Sally caught my eye, and she looked panicked in a way I wasn't going to be able to ignore, no matter how much I would have wanted to.

"We can't leave before the brunch, Leon." She turned to me. "Roxy, tell him. We are all signed up to be a part of the brunch, and mother wants this to be a final family gathering before we all head home. Who knows when we'll be able to get together again like this? We can't leave early just because you think you have some all-important businessman stuff to do. I specifically asked for this full week off, and you promised it to me. Now, do what you promised, or there will be consequences the likes you've never seen. Walter already left, so at least we don't have to deal with that imbecile. If you try to leave now, it will be your life and my money on the line. Don't forget that."

Whoowee, that was pointed, and I had never wanted to excuse myself to go look for a notecard so badly in my life.

It sounded like she mumbled something under her breath about her husband being the only imbecile she still had to endure. Since I couldn't swear to it, and I wasn't going to mention it if Leon hadn't heard it, I kept it to myself.

So much for the fun family week that I'd thought they'd all had. Things were not always as they seemed. I knew that, but was still surprised to see it happen right before my eyes. I needed to get that card and get them out of here before things blew up. The sooner the better, apparently, before someone ended up dead from the daggers flashing in Sally's eyes.

Chapter 2

I t had been over six months since our last murder in our small town, and I did not want to be a witness to another. They were in a staring showdown, and I was almost afraid to blink in case something happened.

He looked away first, and she nodded quickly and decisively.

Okay, so I read that wrong, obviously not panicked, or at least that was not what her voice and her words were telling me, even if her eyes still looked a little wild. If I'd had a book in my hand, I would have consulted it quickly, just to get a read on the situation. Unfortunately, I had nothing at my disposal, so I just clasped my hands at my waist and smiled at the couple.

"I do know that Penny was very much looking forward to this meal, and Glennis has been working all morning on getting the perfect recipe." Make that finding what she thought was the perfect recipe, but I wasn't going to tell them that, either.

Just then, Aunt Hellen breezed through the front doors at my back, followed closely by my Uncle Vince. They weren't related in any way, since one was related to my dad and the other to my mom, but that might change here soon. I smirked at the way they were both coming in at the same time, and Aunt Hellen seemed to be in the same clothes she'd had on last night.

That was truly none of my business. However, she could take care of this now, and that would be her penance for staying out all night.

"Oh!" she said as she stopped staring longingly into Vince's eyes and seemed to finally realize that there were people in the lobby. "Leaving already? I'm certain Glennis is hard at work in the kitchen putting together the most divine meal for you. I promise you that you won't want to miss it."

And with that, she went behind the counter, flipped the computer on, and kept smiling as Vince moved toward the dining room, holding up a very familiar box.

"Donuts to the sideboard, and I got the good kind!"

Leon Mitchell, Sally's husband, sighed and pinched the bridge of his nose, then groaned.

"We're not leaving early. Don't try this again." Sally followed along behind Vince, asking which bakery he'd gotten the donuts from, leaving Hellen and me staring at each other as Leon stalked down the hallway and then mounted the stairs to the second floor. His shoes pounded on the stairs like he wanted to punish them for carrying him up to the room he'd had for the last week. As long as he didn't break the banister or punch a hole in the wall, we were good to go. The stairs had seen a lot of action over the years. They could handle a little temper tantrum.

With that issue put to rest, I now had an obligation to razz my Aunt Hellen about her night out. I never missed a chance if I could help it. Especially when she was acting as she was now, doing everything she could to avoid my eyes. Yes, I had a recipe to find, but this opportunity wasn't going to come again any time soon, and it might just be time to poke at her.

"So nice of you to show up," I said, moving casually toward the front desk counter where Aunt Hellen was making it look like she was doing all kinds of things, like shuffling papers, rearranging the stapler, and fluffing up the cup of pens. The counter was an old oak monstrosity that had stood in the same place for almost one hundred years. I'd never considered taking it down, because it meant so much to the inn. Though I had been thinking about bringing in a craftsman to make sure it would hold up for another hundred years.

"I'm right on time if you'd check your watch, and last I heard, no one was supposed to be leaving for another two hours. Malcolm and Harvey aren't even here to do their porter duties, so don't give me grief, okay?"

I didn't give her grief, but I did give her the side-eye in the pause before I decided on my own to move on to the next subject. "Glennis lost the recipe for the breakfast she was making for this morning, and apparently, there is no way to replace it. She's beside herself. I'm looking for it so no one else has to deal with her attitude."

"Lost the recipe? Isn't that the one that's been in her family since ye olde times of yore? How does she not know how to make that without a piece of paper? The woman can whip up a complicated soufflé with her eyes closed and one hand tied behind her back." Aunt Hellen tucked her dark hair behind one ear.

I lifted my shoulders in a shrug, then tapped a finger on the counter. "Do you think that if I look at the books, they might tell me what happened to it?" I was still learning this talent that I'd been given at birth. I'd always thought it was the lamest of talents to ever grace our family of very cool talents, but it had come in handy over the last few months, so I was making an effort to really learn how to harness it. Long ago, Vince and Hellen should have taken me in hand and taught me all I needed to know, but some kind of disagreement had kept them from doing anything more than shepherding me along and putting up guard rails if I strayed too far from the path.

We'd been working on that, but lately they'd been going off on their own path by making googly eyes at each other. They most likely thought they were being secretive, or at least discreet about it, but they were incredibly wrong. Or at least ignorant about the fact that everyone and their sister could see what was happening.

And speaking of sisters...here came Mena, running down the stairs like the carpet was on fire. I double-checked just to make sure that was not actually true and released a breath when she came to a full stop at the bottom of the stairs. Typical Mena, she struck a pose with her hand on the newel post and the other anchored to her hip. "It's almost vacation time! Are you ready to get this thing rolling?"

Boy, was I ever, but first we had to get through the brunch and get everyone out the door with no more arguments or mishaps. "When do you leave?"

She was heading out to spend some time on the road with our parents, who pretty much lived in their travel trailer, taking the scenic route to everywhere most of the year. I adored them and was happy when they came into town, but just as happy when they left to run around in all their glory.

"They should be here this afternoon," she said. "I figured that way it would be easier to get the trailer into the parking lot without all the cars from the guests."

"Appreciated."

She beamed her smile at me, the one that was literally filled with magic. It didn't always work on me like it did on other people, but I was willing to let down my guard and get infiltrated by her sunshine this time.

"Anything for my sister," she said.

"Anything, but making sure your dishes are in the washer when you decide to have a midnight snack," I responded with a smirk. I'd found her bowl and spoon in the sink this morning, rinsed, but not actually put into the washer itself. How could someone not finish the last step on a simple job like that?

Her return smirk was more powerful. It always had been. "Just think, for a whole week you won't have to complain, well, about me at least. I'm sure you'll find something, but at least I'll be taken off the board of possible irritants."

I scoffed. "I'm sure there'll be something that you forgot to do around here before leaving that I'll have to clean up. If your ears are burning, it will be because I found it and am complaining."

At that, she laughed and then rushed over to hug me. Being the middle child did have its advantages. I was older than her, but not the oldest, so we were close yet still able to have battles that inflicted little to no pain while still clearing the air.

Before she had come back, I hadn't seen her in a long time. Then she'd shown up in town on a job as a nanny for the family staying here a few months ago. I hadn't realized how much I'd missed her until she'd come laughing out of the kitchen. And as much as I looked forward to having the place and Dean to myself, I knew I would miss her. I hoped she came back instead of remembering the fun of being on the road as a dog sitter to her many friends. I didn't have my hopes up necessarily, but I was cautiously optimistic that she'd come back and stay, at least for a little while longer.

"Until then, do you mind checking on Clara and Taylor in the dining room? I'm on the hunt for a missing recipe that Glennis apparently cannot live without. She thinks someone swiped it from the kitchen last night. You didn't happen to see it when you had ice cream, did you?"

"I didn't see a card on the counter, but then I wasn't looking. Sorry. I'll look in on Clara and Taylor, though. Auntie Hell, I'll check in with you before I go to see what souvenirs you'd like from my road trip. Don't let me forget." Then Mena took herself off to the dining room to do as I asked, and I got back down to sniffing out clues as to where this recipe could possibly be.

"Why don't you go ahead and check the library?" Aunt Hellen asked. "The recipe could possibly be in those old cookbooks you have stacked on the far wall. Or maybe someone had it stuck to their shoe and tracked it in there. And while you're in there, you could certainly ask a book to help guide you. We went over the steps last week, so it might be time to put some effort into practicing what you're being taught."

How lovely to be brought to task for something I hadn't done wrong. Then again, she was right that I hadn't been doing much to practice the things we'd been going over. On the one hand, I did run an inn. On the other hand, I did have time, but I just wanted to have the fireworks and the glittering words that I had experienced the last time there had been real trouble around here. Because I wasn't getting that anymore, I'd let my training drift off, and that was something I'd done wrong. I needed to get back to it even though I hadn't been able to recreate the colorful display since then.

However, if the fireworks display had only been because we were trying to solve a murder, I would just remember it fondly. I did not want another murder if that was the price I, and the victim, had to pay. No, thank you.

Off to the library I took myself. Uncle Vince had just walked into the lobby, and there was only so much sly innuendo and fawning I could handle before I said something that I probably shouldn't say, or laugh at their ridiculousness when we all knew what was going on.

Not a thought I wanted trailing me to the library. So, I shut it down and made the trek along the hallway to the library, my favorite room in this entire establishment. In fact, it had been since I was little. Sitting at the back of the inn, it had walls and walls of shelves of books, my favorite things in the world. When I'd taken over the inn from Poobah, I'd also installed a rolling ladder much like Belle's in *Beauty and the Beast* because I'd dreamed of one for years. It hadn't exactly worked as I thought it would when I went to swing from left to right on it, and that was all the information I was going to share about that debacle.

Moving on.

The double doors were made of a beautiful walnut that had been carved a lot of years ago by my great-grandfather, times about seven. He'd built the room for his wife, the woman I descended from, the woman who had given up the life she had been told to have through her family. Instead, she'd disappeared on her trip to an arranged marriage and stayed in this small town on the river for her whole life, raising a family with a man who let her be who she was, instead of the man who would have expected her to snuff out her powers in order to fit into his world.

If you looked closely at the right panel, her husband had carved a silhouette of her face into the wood right at the height of his heart. Someday, I dreamed of having a love like that.

Except that if we were being really honest here, I actually had never really given that kind of love a thought. My parents had it, my grandparents had it throughout the years before my grandmother passed, and my oldest sister had it. For me, I had always been so focused on making the inn mine that I had studied and planned and apprenticed, never thinking that I'd do more than be here, taking care of the building and the people who graced us with their presence for short periods of time.

I loved getting to know people on the weekends they stayed here. Having a rotating schedule of short-term friends and ac-quaintances, having them float in and out of my atmosphere, had worked for me for years. But then I'd met Dean when he'd moved to town to take care of the ferry, and I'd dreamed, just for a minute, until I was certain that nothing would ever happen there. So, I'd made peace with just having a constant best friend. Until things changed again, and I'd gotten a kiss that rocked my world.

One of the happiest days of my life was also one of the scariest, but everything since then had been wonderful, at least between us. We did have another death in the last several months, so not everything was light and love. But I wasn't going to think about that.

I traced the silhouette in the door and took a deep breath. Hopefully, I would be able to find this recipe, posthaste, and get it back to Glennis so she could calm herself down. She'd been in a snit pretty much the whole time this family had been here, but I figured that had been because they had not let her cook for them. With any luck, once I got the recipe for her, and she was able to make a fabulous brunch for the Deitz clan, she'd be able to go on vacation, maybe get her drink on, or refill her well, doing whatever she was planning on doing during her week away. And then she could come back closer to how she normally was. Still irritating and lofty, but less insufferable. It was something to wish for at least.

Our first few months as boss and employee, instead of two employees under Poobah, had been pretty good, but something had happened recently that made her more combative and not as easy to bring her back to center.

Twisting the brass knob on the left door, I let myself into the library and then closed it softly behind me. After this morning in general, I myself needed a few seconds to get back to center. And this was the perfect place to do that. It was filled with groupings of chairs, beautiful tables, and sconces galore. The lights were on a low setting right now, since it was still morning. They were set to flare brighter in an hour or so, but I'd be out of the room by then. I'd have to be, or I'd be able to hear Glennis scream all the way down here as she made a still awesome, but to her a second-rate, casserole for breakfast.

I leaned back against the double doors and breathed deeply. I could do this.

I was good at finding things, usually, and I was not against doing whatever I had to do in order to keep my excellent cook happy. I just took a second, though, to wish that it didn't have to be so difficult sometimes. Why couldn't she bend?

It was a question with no good answers. So, I pushed away from the door and got ready to look high and low for that dang card. I hadn't even asked if it was written on a card or a piece of paper. I tried to envision what it looked like and couldn't come up with anything. I'd know it when I saw it, of course, but until I saw it, I was operating at a serious deficit.

Starting at the floor and the shelving nearest me, I searched every inch that I could see, running my hand over book spines and the space in front of the books. Thank goodness I didn't have white gloves on because it became apparent pretty quickly that we needed to get in here and do some real dusting. Oops.

But that was a problem for a different day. Walking my fingers over the last inches of the first shelf, I then focused on the carpet. It probably would be a good idea to vacuum in here, too. That would be on the cleaning crew's list of things to do, regardless. But the kids in the family had been playing in here a lot over the last week, so there were bound to be some crumbs on the floor. They could be dealt with easily enough before everyone left for vacation.

I moved to the next shelf and started the same routine I'd done on the first shelf. This was going to take forever. I loved all the books in here normally and could have lived in this space alone if I'd had to, but searching every single nook and cranny of the place was not high on my list of desires at the moment. Not to mention, Glennis was probably about at the point where she was going to lose her lid. I couldn't afford for her to throw her apron on the prep table again and decide she was done.

There was, of course, another way to do this. I grabbed a book off the shelf in front of me and then closed my eyes. Centering myself was usually easy, but I had found that if I concentrated on that and asked a specific question, I generally got better answers. Or at least a better answer than just throwing a question out into the Universe, while hoping someone else might be able to interpret what exactly I was asking for, and then give me the answer I needed, one that would make sense to me.

Leaning my forehead on the shelf in front of me, I stuck my finger in the book and breathed. "Please tell me what I need to know. Help me to help Glennis in the very best way possible. What is the best way possible to help Glennis? Where is the recipe card?"

Nothing wrong with covering all the bases I could think of.

I opened the book and closed my eyes as I traced a finger down the very old page. I'd picked something from the classics section and hoped that would work in my favor.

My eyes scanned the paragraph and came up with nothing. I read it again, and it was like I didn't have any talent at all. The words themselves made sense. The sentence was structured correctly, and the way it sounded when I read it out loud made the words sound like they belonged together, but there was no click in my brain that would interpret them in a way to answer my question.

Argh!

I heard what could have been a quiet sigh or hum behind me, and then the letters rose off the page, sparkling as they hadn't in a very long time. I dreaded reading the message after the connection between trouble and sparkling letters I'd made earlier, but I couldn't ignore the message that the Universe was sending me just because I didn't want to see it. Maybe an animal had chewed up the card, and it was gone forever. I did not want to go to Glennis with that information, but it would be better than the last time the letters had lit up like a fireworks display on the Fourth of July.

Finally, I forced my eyes open, braced myself against the shelf with one hand on the solid wood, and looked at the message floating above the book.

Look Behind You

Did I have to?

I won't lie. I closed my eyes and stood where I was for another few seconds. I kept my eyes closed, too, when I finally got to the point where I could turn around. This could just be a clue as to where the recipe card was. Maybe the book was telling me that the card was on the floor behind me. Perhaps all I needed to do was turn around and look behind me, and I'd find the small piece of cardboard or paper. Maybe it was under a couch, or under a table, or maybe it had gotten stuck under the edge of the carpet that was hidden under the cabinet that I'd recently found in the back of the cellar.

Of course, I wouldn't know until I actually opened my eyes. I took another three seconds and then grunted at my own procrastination and opened my eyes.

And that's when I saw Penny Deitz slumped over in a chair by the fireplace, and there was no way she was still alive.

So much for thinking those sparkling letters didn't have anything to do with major problems.

Chapter 3

Oh, man...oh, man...oh, man...oh, man...this was not good. What on earth had happened to her? Her eyes were glassy, and she was slumped over to the right, nearly hanging off the edge of the chair. She obviously was not breathing. Oh, man.

I crept toward her, even though it wasn't like I was going to scare her or anything. She was way beyond ever being scared again.

Oh, man.

I did take in the scene for a moment, as I placed my fingers at her throat to see if there was a pulse, while I tried to let my brain get on track with what I was seeing here. Yes, she was slumped over. Yes, her eyes were glassy. I watched for about thirty seconds to make absolutely certain her chest wasn't moving at all to indicate any breathing. Her arm dangled toward the ground. Her clutch purse was attached at the wrist with a heavy leather loop that looked like it had seen better days.

Since I loved antiques, my brain decided to focus on the fact that it was a designer bag from back in the forties. Really, I should not have been so focused on that when I had a dead woman in front of me, but I couldn't stop myself.

Had she died of natural causes? From what I knew, she was in her mid to late sixties and spry, but that didn't mean there weren't things going on inside her body that we just couldn't see on the outside. No one had said anything on the forms about any allergies or health complications that we should be on the lookout for. The form was completely voluntary and only offered as a way to assist if something were to happen at the inn. But now I was trying to remember what she had said, and what thing, other than murder, this could be.

That all became irrelevant when I noticed the trail of blood dripping down her forehead. Through her fringy, dyed-brown hair, I could see a major cut, almost a dent, right at her hairline. One that matched the candlestick holder resting in her lap. Oh, no. This was the complete opposite of good, and I was going to be sick.

What in the weird? I stifled a scream, even as it seemed to be trying to claw its way out of my throat.

With wild eyes, I looked around the huge room. Where had the candlestick holder come from? The mantle? On one of the end tables? Was the person who had struck her so violently still here in the library? Had the sigh I heard before the letters sparkled above the page come from her? Had it actually been a groan, or a moan of death, finally claiming her?

Not wanting to make the same mistake I had made last time, I quickly moved to check her pulse again to make sure that there was no way she could be saved. She felt cold to the touch, which made me think that there was no way she had just groaned and then died. She would have had to be dead for some time to be cold to the touch. Wouldn't she? I thought so.

Regardless of her temperature, though, I had to call the cops. Now.

And I didn't have my phone with me. Crap! Penny's purse hanging from her wrist caught my eye. If her phone was in there, it probably wasn't password-protected, and if it was, then I'd go out into the hall and ask Aunt Hellen to place the dreaded call. I so did not want the cops out here again.

I made a grab for her purse, and the clasp popped, spilling the contents on the floor. And there was the recipe card.

Oh, man.

"Roxy, you in here?" Dean. Dean was in the doorway.

I closed my eyes on the thought that I wished he had waited just a few more seconds, because then I could have shoved the recipe card in my bra. It was a very Poobah thing to consider. Not that he had a bra, but that he would have taken it to hide the evidence that could possibly point a finger at one of our employees, at least until he could figure out if she'd actually killed her. Then again, if Glennis had killed for the recipe, why hadn't she taken it with her?

My brain was awhirl with so many thoughts when really I should have only been thinking of one thing. "Do you have your phone on you?"

"Yeah, it's right here."

"Call the police. Something happened to Penny, and we need them out here right away."

He started dialing and then made eye contact with me. "Something that they should rush the EMTs out here for because they could save her if we weren't talking right now?"

All I did was shake my head.

"Damn." He hit the last number and put the phone up to his ear.

"Yeah," I said, feeling like the recipe card was burning a hole in the rug. I considered grabbing it, even though it was a very wrong thing to do, but Dean barely blinked as he stared at me with the phone up to his ear.

He never took his eyes off me as he explained the situation and then hung up. "They'll be here shortly. Until then, we're not to leave the room, and we aren't allowed to let anyone in. Who knows you're in here? And who is expecting you to come back any time soon?"

I gulped. "Aunt Hellen is out at the main desk. She sent me back here to see if…" I gulped again. Was I going to lie? I couldn't do it. There were already so many things I couldn't tell him, like anything about my talent, and I wasn't going to add to that list. I leaned over again to check her pulse for a third time and looked longingly at the recipe card on the floor, then I used the toe of my shoe to push it under the chair. It wasn't where I wished it would be, but it was much better than being in my bra.

I cleared my throat and straightened up. "She sent me back here to get a book." That was the truth, insofar as I was here to find a book to see if it would answer my question of where the recipe was, or to find a book that contained the recipe that was missing. Fortunately, I knew without a shadow of a doubt that Aunt Hellen would go along with any story I told. But like I said before, I did not want to lie, and this at least was partially true. It was going to have to be enough. Dean was right to use the word damn the first time, and I was going to reiterate it. Damn.

"Okay, let's not move anything or do anything until they get here."

"Makes sense." I looked back over at Penny and the gash in her head. "Mrs. Deitz, in the library, with a candlestick. That's awfully *Clue* of them, isn't it?"

Dean gave a shocked snicker and then turned it into a cough when Norm came busting through the door. The cop came in hot, hitting Dean with the door so hard that he almost crashed into the wall before righting himself.

"Where is she, and what did you do?" Norm came to a standstill about a foot from me, huffing as if he had run.

"Where did you come from?" I asked, taking a step back to get out of his sucking and blowing strike zone.

He patted his thinning, light hair and stuck a hand to his chest. "Doesn't matter, and I'm not going to answer it, even if it did. I'm the one asking the questions here, and my first is, how do you seem to keep finding these bodies? You're lucky that the other two had definite killers, but at some point, if you keep finding all these bodies, someone's going to wonder if you might be a serial killer. You ever think about that?"

Well, I wouldn't be able to not think about that now. There was a need for that word damn again.

"I had nothing to do with this," I shot back. "I came in to find a book, and when I turned around..." Because the book had told me to, but I wasn't going to add that part in for him. "I found her slumped over in the chair. It looks like someone hit her on the head with a candlestick."

"Someone killed her in the library with the candlestick." He shook his head. "So, are we looking for Professor Plum?"

I would not give him points for the same *Clue* reference I had made earlier. Would. Not.

"That's what you're going with, Norm?" Dean asked, so I didn't have to.

"Things are crazy around here, Dean. We've never had so many murders in just under a year, and somehow they are all connected with the inn. I'm just trying to keep my sanity in the midst of all this."

Fair enough, but again, I was not going to be nice to him just because he briefly looked as lost as I felt in this storm. He'd revert to his jerky self in a few seconds. I could feel it in my bones and didn't have to ask a book for that prediction.

"I'll need to talk to everyone on the staff, as well as all your guests." Norm took a handkerchief out of his pocket and wiped his brow, even though it was exceptionally cool in here.

My guests! Oh, my word! This was so much worse than my mind had registered when I first saw Penny in the chair. Then,

I was just concerned about what had happened to her and who had done it. But Norm mentioning wanting to talk to my guests also just pinged in my brain that her whole family was here. They were supposed to be leaving after brunch. Would there even be a brunch? Would they want brunch at all when they heard that their relative had been murdered?

My black cat, Mustafa, Moose for short, came strolling in from somewhere at the back of the library and immediately went under the chair where Penny lay dead.

"Moose," I hissed, and he gave me side eye like you could not even imagine. I tried again anyway. "Moose! Get out of there."

Instead of listening, he started batting around a tube of lipstick, a compact, and a small notebook. After a second or two of that, he went for the recipe card and used his paw to move it back and forth on the carpet.

I bent down to grab him, and Norm jumped in front of me, scaring me into a squeak.

"Don't even think about touching anything," he said with a sneer.

"I was only..." I trailed off when he pushed my shoulder back, and then Dean was there.

"Absolutely not necessary, Norm. Back off. She was trying to secure your crime scene, which you have not done yet, by grabbing her cat so he didn't mess anything up." And he bent down to pick up Moose, who immediately curled up in his strong arms and started purring. I wished I could do the same thing.

There was a split second when I could have taken the distraction and grabbed the card, but just like the first time, I simply couldn't do it. Yes, Glennis was going to be angry that I hadn't grabbed the card off the floor, but she'd just have to get over it. We might not be having brunch at all once the family is told.

How had life become so flipping complicated? I was not on board with this, in case anyone was listening.

With Dean and Moose at my side, I finally looked at Norm again, daring him to touch me one more time. "The guests are only booked through today and are scheduled to check out in a few hours. I'm sure they'll be around until then."

Norm scoffed and ran his hand over his thinning hair again. *Maybe he needed to stop that if he didn't want to lose even more hair.* I kept that thought to myself.

"They'll be around far longer than that, if I have anything to say about it. We're not going to have people skipping town when I might have follow-up questions. And they might not want to scatter to the winds before finding out what happened to their relative."

It wasn't a very nice thought, but I couldn't stop my brain from saying: *There went my vacation.*

"You can't keep them here." Or could he?

"I most certainly can if I think they all have motives or reasons for wanting someone on the premises dead."

My head hurt.

"What is..." The female voice in the hallway trailed off, and then she covered her mouth, but I could still hear her scream. It was Sally from the lobby, Penny's daughter, and things were about to get really bad. Why hadn't Norm put someone on the doorway so no one could come in and see the body now that it had been discovered?

Dean was quick to usher her out into the hallway, Moose still sitting in his arms, and then he closed the double doors behind him. Which left me with Norm, but at least we didn't have the daughter in here wailing.

"You might have wanted to put someone in the hallway so no one could step on your crime scene." I knew I shouldn't have said it as soon as the words left my mouth.

Norm pivoted to me slowly, like he was on one of those rotating tables in the front of the candy store, showing you everything that was available that you could get. And I knew what I was getting was not going to be pretty.

He opened his mouth, but then he snapped it closed to stalk past me and crouch down on the floor at the foot of the chair where Penny was dead. He used a pen to pull the recipe card to him from its resting place. "What is Aunt Glennis's recipe card doing under the victim's chair? Was she in here? Have you been able to verify her alibi for this morning?"

He was winging the questions out so fast that I had no chance to even understand what he was saying, much less answer like a rational adult. I took a deep breath and tried anyway.

"Slow down. I didn't know anyone had died in here until about thirty seconds before you did. I had Dean call you as soon as he walked in because I didn't have my cell with me. It happened very quickly, so no, I haven't verified anyone's alibi at any time. I don't know how the card got under the chair. Maybe it's been there for weeks."

His gaze shot up to my face, and I did everything I could to not squirm. We would have vacuumed in here and found that card at some point.

But he had to know that his aunt would never kill someone. The two women didn't even know each other. And, even if Penny had stolen Glennis's recipe from the kitchen, was that really something that Glennis would have killed over? She could be a pain, and she could do things that made me want to yell, but I couldn't see her as a killer. There was no way her own nephew would either. No way.

And yet, he stalked away without another word to me. He had plenty of words for the cop who was now stationed at the double doors, and he had several words for the woman standing out in the hallway asking what had happened to her mother.

He even had a few for Dean, who was in the process of coming back into the library, just as Norm was returning.

"Don't touch anything and make sure Roxanne doesn't touch anything either," he said, following Dean back into the room.

Almost no one called me that, except for my mom when she was irritated. My mom...they were supposed to be showing up in a few hours to take Mena away to traipse through the wilds of the United States of America via travel trailer. If Penny's family couldn't leave, then I wondered if it was possible that my staff wouldn't be able to leave either. I could see how that could be legally necessary, but most of them had already paid for vacations that I was not going to make them miss just because we had yet one more murder to solve.

"Most of my staff have a place to be next week. You've never kept everyone here before. What's different this time?" I asked Norm.

"For one, this death is on the main floor, where anyone and everyone has access. For two, I've been reprimanded for my handling of the last two cases, and I will not be reprimanded again. Ever. This one is going to be completely by the book, and you will not stand in my way. And if it's my aunt who slammed down the candlestick, then there will be no mercy for her."

"Norm!" Glennis had somehow made it through the gauntlet of officers and Dean before entering the room and stalking over to us.

I made a show of trying to get her not to look at the dead body, but she did anyway.

And then she looked over and saw the card in Norm's hand. She made a grab for it and nearly fell until Dean pulled her back. Norm held the card above his head, and that just made her snarl at him. Well, this was not going well, even I could tell that, and

I tended to sometimes be a little slow on the uptake for these kinds of things.

"I'm going to need you down at the station," Norm said, pointing at Glennis and then hooking a thumb over his shoulder. "I'm willing to let you drive yourself down there, since I don't want my mother to be mad at me for forcing you into the back of a squad car, but I expect you in ten minutes. No delay."

"I need that recipe card, Norm. Hand it over."

I stared at her in disbelief. She was only making this worse for herself. Why wasn't she just shutting up? I glanced over at Dean to see what he thought of this whole thing. All I got back was a shrug.

"I have a feeling this is evidence, so I'll be keeping it." Norm shook out a plastic bag and put the card in it. "And you're down a person at the table, so it's possible no one wants your cooking now anyway."

Ow.

Glennis's eyes went into that slitty form. It was even worse than when it was trained on me. But Norm just turned his back on her and walked out.

"Ten minutes. And don't tell a single person that this is anything more than a death," he said loud enough for everyone in the room to hear, and then he left. A gurney was brought in, and the body was quickly moved out of the room, too.

I glanced at Glennis to see what she'd do next. The absolutely dejected look on her face took me aback. It was just a flash of a moment, and then her whole visage hardened into fury. What was she going to do next?

"Why is this recipe so important to you?" I asked because at this point, it almost had to be something more than the ingredients and the right way to prepare them. It had to be.

"There's a note on the back that is everything to me, Roxy, okay? It's not just the recipe, although that is important, too.

But what's more important is that it's mine. *Mine.* It has been mine for years, and no one is allowed to take that from me."

"Trying to grab it out of Norm's hands didn't do you any favors." I crossed my arms under my chest and gave her room to tell me something more than just that it had a note on it.

"I don't need any favors."

I sighed. "I'm not sure that you're looking at this right. You're being asked to the police station for questioning about your involvement in a murder, Glennis. A recipe card from long before you were born can't be more important than that."

She shook her head at me as if I had no clue. "I'll call my sister on my way to the station. Everything else is ready for brunch if anyone is still interested. I'll be back soon. That I'm going to promise with no doubt. Little brat is about to see what happens when you mess with family, especially his own." She stomped out of the room, shaking off the hand that one of the officers put out. Did he think she was going to let him manhandle her to her own car? Fat chance of that.

I was absolutely itching to open any of the books in the library to see what they might have to say, but there were way too many people in the room. Not to mention Dean was here, and he was the one I most did not want to practice my talent in front of because I couldn't answer any questions he might have.

People started filing out of the library, and I held my breath to see if Dean would follow them out. It would be ideal, no matter how much I wanted to spend every minute with him that I could, I needed to do this on my own. The last time I had sparkles, he'd heard a hum that I couldn't explain. I didn't want to have to do that again, but there were a few sparklers trailing out of the bookcase under the rolling ladder. It was everything I could do not to shove him out the door, flip the lock, and snag the book that was sparkling.

I couldn't do that, and I didn't know when I could. But the faster I could get him to leave, the happier we would all be. Or at least I would be.

As soon as the room emptied, I went to Dean and planted a kiss on him. "I'm going to have to look into this if Glennis is pulled in as a real suspect, you know that, right?" I asked him.

He nodded. "I figured as much."

"Will you be my Watson again?" It was one of the first things the sparkly books had told me, that Dean was my Watson. I had not believed it at the beginning, but each time he had been instrumental in helping with the investigation, and I couldn't do this without him.

"Always." He looped his arms around my waist and pulled me in until we were touching from chest to knees.

"That sounds like a promise."

"The first of many." He kissed me on the nose, and I sighed.

I could stay here forever and was still trying to figure out how to do that. I wanted a life with him, but because he was not "talented," I was never going to be able to tell him about my bibliomancy, or the things I could do with it. So, I would never be able to share with him part of my core life, and I couldn't imagine doing that to him or myself for all the years to come.

During the last murder investigation, though, his niece had shown a few tells on being able to see and do things that some-one who didn't have any talent shouldn't be able to do. Which meant there was a possibility his niece had her own talent. That could open doors that I had considered not even existing, much less possible to open. While it gave me hope, I still hadn't come up with a way to make it happen.

That was a thought for a different time.

For now, I was going to take just another second or two in the arms of the man I loved more than anything in this world, even my talent.

Or that was the plan until someone threw the door open, making it bounce off the interior wall and the bookcase positioned to the left of the entrance. And then ten guys came trooping in with the dirty boots and their evidence cases.

I should have thought about the fact that they were going to be here and grabbed the sparkly book earlier. Dang it! Now I was going to have to come back after they left and hope that the book would sparkle again.

I'd say excellent, but I didn't feel that, no matter how I tried to spin it. Instead, I just thought of the word of the day. Damn.

Chapter 4

With all the police people in the library, and having to figure out how to keep everyone here without telling them what had actually happened in the library, I decided to call a meeting in the dining room. We might as well eat all the food Glennis had prepared and use the beautiful room that Taylor and Clara had spent so much time putting together. I personally knocked on every door upstairs and invited each of the family members down.

We had several singles and a couple of couples, as well as a few rooms with children. This, of course, meant the big table in the dining room was full downstairs within minutes, even without Penny there. Everyone had been told that one of the matriarchs of the family was no longer alive, but no one had told them it appeared to be a murder. After Norm had voiced his instructions on his way out of the library, his second in command, Micah, also let me know that I was not to mention anything about what I'd seen, under any circumstances.

Regardless of what I had been told, I was concerned Sally might be the one to tell her family what she had seen in the library. But it turned out she had only been able to get a quick view of her mother slumped over in that chair, and assumed she'd suffered a heart attack or another natural form of death.

As they all gathered around the table, she sniffled as she expressed how thankful she was that even though Penny had been alone in the room, she had been in the presence of family in the building and in a place that was so important to her.

The mood at the table was definitely sad, but there didn't appear to be much crying, though there were some puffy eyes.

Time to get this thing started.

"I'm so sorry for your loss," I said. "You are more than welcome to stay an extra night at no cost to remain in town and not leave just yet. I'm sure this is difficult for all of you. I don't expect you to just load up your cars and set out for home in the middle of this tragedy."

"Thank you so much, Roxy. We appreciate your graceful hospitality and understanding." That was the other matriarch of the family, Penny's sister, Jessica. "Obviously, this is a difficult time. Penny was a wonderful person who gave to so many other people."

There was a subtle cough from my left, and I wasn't sure what to make of that, or who it came from, but I wasn't given time to think about it because Jessica continued on in her formal speech pattern. I'd dealt with all kinds of people throughout the years, so I was open to the way she spoke, but it was harder to follow than if she had just said what she needed to without dressing it up.

"We, of course, will have her removed to her hometown as soon as possible, but having an extra day to make sense of this loss would be greatly appreciated."

Leon scoffed, and Sally elbowed him hard. He grabbed his upper arm, frowning. Oh, this was going to be fun.

Jessica turned her head away from him and patted the arm of her son next to her. "Michael, we have all the information for the services back at the house, and it should be easy enough to get the funeral set up in a short time. Next week would be best.

Letting her finally get her rest will be a kind of sendoff that she so deserved."

"Will you be reading from part of her memoir at the service? I'm sure that would be lovely," Sally said from the other end of the table.

Every eye at the table turned to her. Well, except for the toddler who was bouncing in his chair and trying to grab as many blueberries as possible to lob at one of his sisters, but that was beside the point. Every other person at the table turned to look at Sally, and I wasn't sure why mentioning a memoir would have created that kind of response.

"That memoir will never see the light of day," Jessica intoned from her place at the head of the table on the other end, spreading her hands on the table in front of her. "It was already destroyed long ago because it was a retelling of something that should never have been told. Nothing good would come of it, nothing good came of it, as it led her to make decisions that were questionable at best, horrendous at worst." She stared her niece down as if she might go against her. Nothing could be further from the truth, it seemed, though, when I looked back at Sally.

Sally, who I found staring at the ceiling as if it held all the answers to life's questions. No one else looked at each other, either. All avoided eye contact with anyone near them or across the table. Everything in the room seemed to suddenly be of huge fascination, from the wallpaper to the light fixtures to the candle arrangement on the table. Except for Leon, who glanced my way with the hint of a smug smile on his face before he placed his hand on top of his wife's on the table and seemed to squeeze.

What was that all about? I had a feeling no one would want to answer that question. But it was going on the top of my list to share with my Watson, just as soon as I could get out of here and start looking into a few things having to do with the untimely death of one Penny Deitz.

The desire to get my hands on that memoir was nearly overwhelming. Was it currently in her room? Could I get into her computer? Did she have it on a computer? Was it all handwritten? I didn't know exactly how old she was, but anything was possible. Maybe she was still using an old typewriter. I wasn't willing to rule anything out at this point.

Who could I ask? I looked around the table, starting with Jessica, and dismissed that as a no. Then there were her two sons, one with a wife and two children, and one by himself. Penny's daughter, Sally, was next, with her husband and their two teenagers, along with a toddler. And Sally was joined by her two sisters and a brother who had all come by themselves.

Which of them would know about the memoir? Which of them might have helped her pull her research? Sally obviously knew enough to mention it, but she must not have been aware that it was destroyed. Unless it wasn't.

I had no idea who was the older sister between Jessica and Penny, or what everyone was like outside their vacation personalities, but I was certain I was about to know all the things about every single person sitting at this table. Especially Leon, who had wanted to leave before brunch, before Penny was found. I wasn't sure how I was going to do the deep dive on each person, or how many days I might have to do it, but I was formulating a plan in my head.

"Again, I'm sorry for your loss and hope that you will let us know if we can help you in any way while you're here. In the meantime, why don't we eat?" I said.

Jessica nodded. "There's no use in letting this beautiful food go to waste." Magically, the pause and avoidance around the table stopped at Jessica's command, and they all dug into the delicious-looking food Glennis had prepared.

There were scones and clotted cream, fresh strawberries, baked cinnamon peaches from one of my favorite childhood books, and a quiche that was filled with eggs, ham, and cheese. I loved Glennis's five-star soufflé as much as anyone else, but the spread she had put out was definitely top-notch. If she had been here, instead of at the police station battling with her nephew, she would have appreciated seeing how everyone dove into the food with an enthusiasm unmatched by anything else they'd done here over the last week.

They should have taken her up on the other meals she could have prepared during their stay. Everything Glennis made was delightful, even more so than the food before them.

She had so many recipes and ways of preparing food, and she usually did it completely without any help from a recipe. I knew now that it wasn't the recipe itself that was so important, but that it was what was handwritten on the back. But what was so important that she would risk going to jail for it? I wished I had turned it over to read the message before deciding not to shove it into my bra, but I hadn't known.

Maybe I'd put in a phone call to Glennis's sister, too, just to see what I could do to help Glennis. And if the opportunity arose to ask about that recipe card, then I wasn't against making some additional conversation along the way.

My list of things to do was growing. I left the dining room and the family to eat away their grief so I could check to make sure everything else was okay in the kitchen. While I was there, I could also grab a piece of paper and start my list of suspects. Of course, I hated to call them that, but persons of interest seemed so cold when I felt like there wasn't anything cold about what had been done to Penny. Actually, there might be quite a few hot-button issues that need to be explored. Leon wanting to leave and overpower "her," and that memoir were just two of them.

It would have to wait, though, because I was not alone in the kitchen when I swung the door open. Clara and Taylor were in there with a stout box sitting on the counter. They were whispering to each other, and I considered just standing there for a second to see if they'd reveal anything without knowing they had an eavesdropper, but I just couldn't do it in the end. I had to be honest with someone to the best of my ability. I was going to be skulking around enough until I figured out who had killed Penny. I didn't need to do it when it wasn't warranted. At least not yet.

"Hey there!" I let the door swing shut behind me and then walked over to the cookie jar. I had viewed all that awesome food in the next room and hadn't touched a single thing, so I deserved something for my restraint. I drew out one of Glennis's super double chocolate love-bomb brownies and set it on a plate on the counter, then dug around in the drawer for a plastic fork.

"You didn't snag a donut from Vince's offerings on the sideboard?" Clara asked.

"Dang it. I didn't even think about those!"

"We kind of figured since we watched you go into the dining room, but came out empty-handed."

And that I had also forgotten, just for a second. I could watch the family from the monitor on the wall to the right, and they'd have no idea. I couldn't listen to them because there was no audio, but sometimes body language was far better than actual language.

Leon was gesticulating wildly, but his mouth was not opening very much. So, was he talking low, but unable to keep himself from acting out the pieces of what he was saying? Then again, he could have been telling a joke. I had to stop being so negative about everything.

Except Sally turned away from him with her arms clamped hard around her midsection, and his daughters ignored him altogether. Jessica looked ready to spit fire, and her other daughter frowned and then flattened her lips in a hard line.

Okay, the body language was bad, but I still wished I could hear what they were saying.

"I should go back in and snag a donut before they're all gone."

Clara grabbed my forearm. "I'd let whatever is going on in there play out and wait to see what happens next. Taylor and I were talking about it, and we're pretty sure you're not going to be able to let this go if Glennis has the gavel dropped on her for something she probably didn't do."

"Probably?" I said, catching on to her phrasing.

"Most likely?" Clara raised her hands and shrugged. "I've seen that card before, and she never lets anyone turn it over. It has to stay on the counter, just as it is, and you are *not*, under any circumstances, to touch the thing. I asked once why she didn't just copy it over onto a different piece of paper and leave the original at home if she was that concerned, but she was totally against that. She probably went ballistic when she couldn't find the thing this morning, but without knowing who had it or where it was, she just stood in here and banged some pots and pans around. That's why I say she *probably* wouldn't have hurt anyone for the card." She paused. "She didn't hurt anyone, did she? Our understanding is that the matriarch is dead. Did someone help her along to that place?"

Technically, I had sworn to Micah that I wouldn't say anything to the family, and these two weren't in the family I'd sworn about. Plus, they were my staff and here a lot, so if they had to be on the lookout for things, or maybe knew something that would only be triggered by me sharing information, then I had no other choice. I'd defend that to my dying day. Hopefully, it wouldn't get that far, though.

"She was killed in the library with a candlestick."

"That was awfully *Clue* of them, wasn't it?" Taylor said and then slapped a hand over her mouth as her shoulders shook in mirth. Clara didn't have the same restraint, and she chuckled. I couldn't blame her.

"I know it's not funny," Taylor said. "Sorry, but that's just really weird. The family's been here this whole week. Why wait until the last minute to decide to kill someone right before you're going to go home? Especially since they had a brunch scheduled, so it wasn't like she wouldn't have been expected at the table. No one thought she had already checked out, so then they all leave, and we find her in the library and have no idea of the timeline?"

"All very good points," I said as I ripped a paper towel from the roll hanging under a cabinet, then swiped a marker off the counter. I could have sworn we normally had pads of paper in here, but the ideas were flying so fast I couldn't wait to find them to write things out, or I'd forget them all.

I scribbled some things down and hoped I'd be able to read them later. If not, then maybe Dean could.

"Have you noticed anything off about the people in the room?" I asked.

"Not really," Taylor said. "I did hear the couple with the wild-haired guy fighting one afternoon as they were coming down the stairs." She pointed at the screen.

Leon again. I hadn't paid too much attention to him and Sally, since I was more concerned about the kids running around. I'd also been focused on making sure I got to spend time with Dean as much as I could instead of what the married couple was doing. I had a feeling I was about to change that while they remained here.

Speaking of them being here, I had to solve this as soon as possible because I didn't know what would happen if Norm demanded the whole family stay here until he found the culprit. Who would pay for that? I was okay with an extra night, especially since they hadn't taken advantage of the other meals we offered, even though they were part of the stay. That choice meant I had saved a ton of money by not having to feed them breakfast at the bed and breakfast. But a week of breakfast wasn't equivalent to having them stay for another several nights, especially if they were going to take advantage of the food now, like they didn't before.

I really hoped Norm wasn't going to make them stay too long.

As if to mock me, guess who I saw walking up through the back yard? Why was Norm coming this way? Where had he parked to get to the backyard at all? Who had let him in?

His gaze was traveling all over the back of the house, over and over. He looked a little like he was about to have a mental breakdown, and I did not have time for that.

I whipped the back door open and called his name. He rested his index finger vertically on his lips, like he was shushing me, and I rolled my eyes.

He picked up the pace and came up even with the door within seconds. When he tried to step through the doorway, I barred his way.

"What exactly are you here for, and why didn't you knock on the front door?"

"Can I please come in before we start talking?"

"I don't think so. I'm going to need you to answer those questions, think of it like buying a pass into the house through the back door."

He grunted at me, but he had no right to force his way in, and so often I was at a disadvantage in our interactions. I was not letting the opportunity to have the upper hand go this time without using it to the best of my advantage.

"Fine, I'm here because I have things to talk about with you. I'm using the back door because I didn't want to have to walk around front just in case I had to see your grandfather."

"He could have been here. How did you know he wasn't?"

"Roxy, why do you have to be like this? Just let me in, and we'll talk about things."

"I don't think I will. You took your own aunt to the station, you have been mean to me for years, and it's only been worse since I found the first dead body. I didn't want to be involved in that, and yet you treated me horribly from day one."

"If I apologize, will you let me in?"

"Will you mean it?"

He groaned and smacked himself in the forehead. "Just let me in, or I can go around front and knock on the door there. Your aunt can answer the door and stare me down like she always does. Then we can exchange words, and I'll have to come back, because I'll be irritated, and this could have all been avoided if you had...just...let...me...in."

"This could have been avoided if you had...just...stopped...being...a...j—"

"Roxy, please let him in," Glennis said from behind me. "I'm back. I don't have my recipe card, because somehow they think it is serious that they found it under her chair, but they said they will keep it safe, and then they let me go."

I had never heard her sound so tired. Even when we had a full house and people wanting food every hour, she was still peppy, saucy, and spicy. But now, she looked like a burned-out husk of herself.

Turning to look her over, I found that she looked just as tired as she sounded. What on Earth had they done to her?

Clara grabbed a stool from the broom closet, and Taylor started the teapot. I frowned at Norm, but I jerked my head at him to tell him to come in.

I had far more questions than just the two I'd started with. And the first was the most important. "Do you honestly think your aunt is capable of killing someone?"

He leaned against the far counter and pinched the bridge of his nose. "I can't afford to make a mistake here, Roxy."

"That's not an answer, and you should be addressing Glennis, not me. You can't honestly think that your own aunt would do something so horrendous, even over a recipe card that's apparently so important to her."

"I know that, and honestly, I don't want to have to ask her questions, and no, I don't actually think she did this, but I also can't show favoritism, and I can't just give her a pass because we're related. I wasn't kidding when I said that I got seriously reprimanded for the last two murder cases and how they went down. I have to do this completely by the book this time, which means talking to each and every person who was on the premises during the crime."

"Can you at least do that here? I already told the family they can stay an extra night, instead of needing to leave right now. They're in the next room eating brunch." I pointed to the big screen above our heads. "Are you going to tell them that it was a murder, or are you going to keep up the cannot confirm or deny schtick?"

"It's not a schtick. I wish you'd take this more seriously." He straightened and folded his arms over his chest. "This isn't a game, or some kind of binge-worthy show, or one of the books you can't seem to put down. This is my job, and our community means a lot to me, so I'd like it to be safe. It's not safe if we have a murderer running around."

"Fair enough."

"That's all you have to say?" he asked.

I chose to nod, much like Glennis had earlier, because if I didn't have anything nice to say, then I was not going to say anything at all at the moment. I'd save it for later, if I still felt he needed to hear it.

"Look, Norm, I appreciate that you need to do your job," Glennis interjected. "And, of course, I want you to be respected at your job. You're good at what you do. I'll answer questions and do what you need me to do, but I also have a job and need to make sure that I'm doing that, too. Now, why are you here, and why did you come in the back door instead of through the front?"

Same questions as I had asked. We'd see if he'd answer them this time.

"You said that you'd been at the inn all morning during the interview, but when I talked to Malcolm, he said that he had seen your car leave the parking lot at seven this morning when he was walking here. He'd thought he was supposed to be here earlier this morning. When he finally checked his calendar, because his alarm hadn't gone off to signal the start of his walk, he realized that he thought it was Saturday and not Friday. He wasn't due for a few hours. So, he went back home, and you passed him. He waved to you, but you appeared to be yelling in the car with the windows up and didn't wave back. He said he was concerned about you. When he tried calling your cell, you never picked up any of his calls."

Glennis looked away, then grabbed a glass from the cabinet above her head. Were we going to do this again? She didn't clink it down this time, so that was something, but she also didn't say anything, which left Norm looking like he was losing patience.

"Where were you headed?" he asked.

"Nowhere."

Well, at least she had answered.

"Aunt Glennis, seriously, I have to know where you were headed, even if it was the pharmacy or something. The stories don't gel, and they need to or I'm not going to be able to take you off my list of suspects."

He sounded defeated, and I felt that in my soul. What was going on that she'd rather lie and protect it than be honest and get herself off the hook? Unless whatever she had to say would very much not get her off the hook and would instead have her dangling for all of eternity.

Or at least until she stopped breathing...

Chapter 5

T his woman was going to be the death of me. "Glennis, you need to tell him what you were doing. He's trying to help you, but you're making it impossible."

She scoffed. "He needs to find the real killer, and then it won't matter where I was and what I was doing." She pointed a scolding finger at him. "Why don't you concentrate on catching the actual perpetrator instead of harassing me?" And she stalked out of the kitchen with her empty cup in hand.

Norm leaned his head back against the wall and released a heavy sigh. I felt that in my soul, too.

"So, has it ever worked to force Glennis to do anything?" I asked, pulling a teacup from the cupboard and using some of the hot water Taylor had started for Glennis.

He laughed derisively. "To be honest? No. She is forever her own person, and while I haven't known her all her life, she's known me all of mine, and that can make things difficult. She'll dig in, and there is nothing, not even dynamite, that can move her. It's frustrating as hell."

"Welcome to my kitchen." I dunked my tea bag a few times and then doused the whole thing with sugar and milk. "So, what do we do?" I knew I was asking a loaded question by using we, but he had to know I was not going to let him take my head cook, chief creator of my kitchen, in if he couldn't find the real person. Which meant I was going to help, whether he liked it or not.

"I don't want it to be her either," he said. "But I have to know for sure."

"Of course. And I can help with that, if you would let me, instead of being a jerk, like you have been in the past."

"I haven't been a-"

I snapped my eyes to him, and he stopped talking immediately. "Are you certain you want to finish that sentence?"

"Okay, look, I wanted to keep everyone safe, and let's be honest, this is all new to me, and it's much different than studying it, or even doing the simulations. There's a lot of pressure, and I don't want to get it wrong."

"But I can help."

He was shaking his head from word one. "I don't want help."

"That's on you then because there is no way I'm not going to help on this one. You weren't wrong that this is a third death linked to the inn and to the people who are either staying here or working here. I don't know if there's anything that makes them all connected or if it's just a weird coincidence, but I can't let it go. I will try really hard not to get in your way, but I'm going to look into things." And that didn't even include what I would hopefully be able to do with the books and my talent. I was going all out this time because it wasn't a clear-cut case of Glennis absolutely absolved, and it needed to be.

"I can't stop you." There was that dejected tone again.

"You won't want to, Norm. I'm not going to solve it. You can do that. I'm just going to make sure that it's not Glennis, and I have far more access to people and things than you do. Why wouldn't you want that?"

"I've explained that before."

"And yet here we are again, and I still don't know what your answer means. So, just let me do what I do, and you do what you do, and we'll meet somewhere in the middle, hopefully soon, with a killer that will confess, and you can be the hero."

"I don't need to be the hero."

"You won't be able to deny it."

He shook his head. "Whatever. If you're going to help, you're going to help. And if that makes it so that this is done by the book, and I don't get reprimanded again for not knowing what I'm doing, then I'm not going to stop you. In fact, help all you want. I have to go back to the station now. But I'll be back this afternoon to do some interviews once I know what I'm looking for and what I need to fill in the gaps." He pushed away from the counter, then hit the swinging door hard enough to have it swing out in a wide arc. Someone on the other side gasped, and I hoped with everything I had that he hadn't just knocked someone into the wall out in the hallway.

That person was Poobah, and fortunately, he had been quick enough to move out of the way. Good, because I had some very pointed questions for him regarding Glennis, and I wasn't going to take avoidance as an answer anymore. Those days were over. He'd better brace himself for the inquisition.

"Can you ladies hold down the kitchen for the next little while?" I asked, turning to Clara and Taylor, who looked both shocked and lost. They were not alone. "I know you've been looking forward to your vacation, and I promise I'm going to do absolutely everything I can to make sure that this goes off at the right time and place. But right now, I need to snag Poobah, and I don't know when Glennis will be back. We don't have anything else to make for a little while, so it should just be a matter of cleaning up once they move on from the dining room." I glanced up at the monitor, and things seemed to have calmed down with everything, no more gesticulating wildly, no wrinkled foreheads. Just stuffing food into their mouths and avoiding each other.

Hopefully, nothing would happen there while I handled my grandfather and finally forced him to tell me what Glennis had on him, and why she felt emboldened enough to not answer questions here or at the police station.

I didn't know where to start looking for him, since he was no longer outside the door. Glancing over at Aunt Hellen in her position behind the front desk, she gestured down the hall to the left. Most likely, he wouldn't be in the library with all the policemen, which meant I would probably find him in the billiards room. There was a dartboard in there, too, and I could either challenge him to a game of pool or dart throwing to force him to answer questions. He couldn't resist either, and I was better than him at both.

Turning the knob to enter the room, I pushed open the door and then held it for a moment to take in what was before me. The pool table was from the 1800s and had been shipped here with the utmost care. It had arrived pristine, then remained that way for all these years with care and polish and oil. Poobah was on the case when it came to making sure that the thing never got over-dry, but also wasn't damp in any way in order to preserve the fabric that allowed the balls to travel smoothly. We'd had a couple of near tears, but part of Poobah's talent was fixing things, and he never had a problem using his reserves to mend anything that ever happened to this beautiful monstrosity. Now, I needed him to mend what was happening at this inn.

"I thought I'd find you here," I said, letting the door slowly swing shut behind me.

"I'm here often enough. The chances were pretty high that you'd be right."

"What is it about the table?" I trailed my fingers along the satin-smooth wood and dipped my hand into the corner pocket where the yellow-striped ball resided. Popping it out, I put it on the table and then moved to the next pocket. From my count, there were six balls missing, all stripes. He must have been running the table before I'd come in. But what had he been doing so close to the kitchen? Close enough to get smacked by the door? Had he been eavesdropping to see what we were saying without entering the conversation himself? Why had he left so quickly? Sneaky, and I wasn't sure I liked that very much.

"It was brought over from a castle that has our family name on it in England. Your great-great-grandfather asked the docent there if we could have it, and then paid way too much money to not only buy it, but also have it shipped here. There was no changing his mind, no matter the price. He wanted this one. He'd gone over to visit the estate to get some insight into the lineage of our family. He was trying to write out the talents and the ways they were used and was told that this table was used long ago as a strategic map."

"A what?"

He spread his hands over the table. "They'd lay all their plans out on here and write on paper with the cloth underneath. If they ever needed to know what was happening, or if someone was taken into custody, they'd be able to place a piece of paper on the table and pick up the indented writing to see who had last used it and for what."

"Holy wow, should we even be playing on this thing? That's amazing!" I hovered a hand over the fabric in awe.

He grinned that grin that he used to break out when he'd done something he was incredibly proud of. "I already got all the notes from the table years ago. I even got a few more than were in the journal from him. He'd missed a couple."

"Can I...Can I see it?" Part of me wondered what would happen if I asked it a question. It wasn't a book necessarily, but it was still the written word, and that had to be worth something to a bibliomancer. Right?

"Let's play for the privilege," he said, taking a cue from the wall. With that smile still in place, he began chalking the tip with the cube he grabbed from the small table jutting out from the wall next to the rack where the various cues hung.

I almost wished he had asked for darts. That would have been faster, and let me get back to sleuthing as quickly as possible. However, until the police were out of the library, there wasn't a ton I could do. And if I could get the book of writings on talents, and how they had been used strategically over the years, and could possibly ask it questions, then holy wow. The holiest of wows that could be awesome!

In my favor was the fact that I was much better at this game than he was, no matter how many years he'd been playing. Lately, I hadn't had time to shoot pool between running the inn and spending time with family, but I could still run the table. I would need to be back here as soon as this mystery was solved, though. I hadn't realized how much I missed it until I picked up my own cue. Maybe I could entice Dean into a game or two. The stakes would be much different, of course, but I could work that all out later.

I racked the balls and set up the cue ball at the end of the table. We'd decide who was shooting to sink what once the triangle of balls was broken and the first ball went into one of the pockets. Classic eight-ball was my favorite. We'd played nine-ball before, and sinking them in numerical order was good. But in this game, I had sometimes run the whole table by pocketing all my balls one after another without giving Poobah a chance to get a single shot in.

"I'm first," I said, setting myself up and making a bridge out of my hand to then rest the cue stick on. As I drew back the cue, I used the time to decide how I was going to hit the ball configuration and where I thought the balls would go.

With a precision I knew I had in me, I hit the white cue ball, striking it just hard enough to break the triangle of solid and striped balls. Hopefully, I'd get stripes and possibly run the table by sinking them all in a series of calculated moves before Poobah even got a chance to do more than watch me win.

I smiled as the striped ten ball sank into the far-left pocket. That meant I still had nine, eleven, twelve, thirteen, fourteen, then fifteen to go before sinking the eight ball and winning. I set my eyes on the twelve and bent over the table to hit the cue ball again, and sank that one, too. Excellent!

"Great job," Poobah said. I glanced over at him, and he was smirking at me. Did he not think I could do this? I'd show him.

I lined up on the fourteen, pulled the stick back, and hit the cue ball straight on with the tip. And missed. Dang it.

"All you." I motioned at the table and stood back, leaning on my cue stick.

"Thanks. You know I always seem to lose to you, but maybe today is my day." He chuckled, and I chuckled with him. He wouldn't be able to do it, but I'd give him the chance.

He had a cluster of three solid balls, the one through the three, on the green cloth of the table. Taking a moment, he moved back and forth at the wood, lining himself up with the cue ball. He pulled the cue stick back too far, and I chalked my tip to be ready for my next chance.

And then all three balls went in separate pockets, one after another. He lined up with the white ball for the next shot, which banked off the buffer, hit the solid four into a pocket, and then glanced off the side of the five ball, which slid right into the far pocket. What the heck?

"Poobah!"

"Shh."

I shushed, but could not believe my eyes.

He had three more to go, and I had six. This had never happened before!

But the last three would not be easy. The six was at the far end of the table, the seven, halfway to us, and the eight was right in the middle of the table.

He leaned over the table, called the balls and which pockets he was going to sink them into, and then pulled back his pool cue. There was no way he'd be able to do that with one shot.

And then he did. Each ball was hit in numeric order, into the pocket he'd called, and then the eight ball glided across the green material and hung on the edge of the right-side pocket. I held my breath, hoping the last one would not drop, wanting to release the breath on the opposite side to see if I could get it to rock back. But then it teetered before falling in. Wow.

"Ha!" Poobah said, pumping his fist into the air, then doing a kind of tap dance with the cue stick like it was a cane and he was Fred Astaire.

"Ha? Really? Ha?" I leaned my cue stick against the wall and ran my hand over the table to check that he hadn't done some kind of magic to win. I felt nothing.

"Oh, yes, ha! I've been practicing and watching videos online every day while you've been running around. Feels good to know that all that practice just paid off."

"What the heck just happened here?" And why did I feel like my whole world had just been turned upside down?

"Oh, my darling. I just couldn't resist breaking the tension you're feeling and putting it into the air. It's practically toxic, even to those who don't have the magic we have. They can still feel it."

I groped behind me for the chair I knew was there somewhere and then flopped into it. I'd lost. To online videos, no less. Or had he always been able to win and had just let me?

"Now, before you dive into some spiral of thinking I've always let you win, please don't. You've always won fair and square, but now that I'm retired and you're running the inn, I had to find some kind of hobby, and I decided that pool was going to be my thing. Thank goodness you didn't push for playing darts. I haven't started that tutorial series yet, but it's next."

I stared at him, trying to take in what he was saying, with my mouth opening and closing.

"You look like a fish out of water, dear. I guess I shouldn't tell you that your grandmother used to cheat when playing War with you by checking her cards to pick one that would just barely win over yours?"

That got me to find my voice. "Yeah, I'd suggest you not mention that right now." I blew out a breath.

"It's not as bad as you think."

"Except that now I don't get the book."

"Yes, but also no. I'll tell you what, you prove that Glennis did not do this, and I'll hand that book right over for you to do your worst."

The giddiness bubbled hard in my belly at his first word, but deflated like flat soda with each new word he said. I had already been signed on to look into things. Somehow, knowing that Poobah was going to be watching and depending on me to not just play at sleuthing, but really hand over the info and the murderer, was a kind of pressure I hadn't felt before.

"She won't even tell me where she was this morning and denied that information to her own nephew, who is just trying to keep her out of jail. She said she wasn't going to tell us anything. According to her, we could just figure out the real killer on our own, which would exonerate her and keep her out of it."

"Oh, now, we might not be able to listen to her on that one. I'll have a talk with her and let her know that I expect her to help out, or there will be consequences."

I squinted at him. "You'd do that? You never do that. She gets away with some pretty unprofessional things sometimes. That was one thing when it was just you, but now that it's me, she still talks to me in a way I would never let anyone else do. It's starting to cause some issues. What does she have on you?"

He didn't even blink at my pointed question. Nor did he answer it. "Let me think on how I'll handle her." He shrugged and seemed to expect me to just go with it.

I was done with this for the last time. "No, I think we're going to have to do a little more than that, Poobah. In fact, you do your thinking, and I'll do mine. Because as much as I love Glennis and want her to stay, I'm not certain that we can keep this up. So put her information in with the book, and I'll agree to look into clearing her name."

"You can't be serious." He put his hands on the edge of the pool table and leaned in.

I mirrored him on my side. "I'm very serious. Think hard about how you want to do this. I'll look into things because it's the right thing to do, and it's not just you wanting me to do this. But I'm going to expect some answers when we're done, or I'll make decisions that you, and she, might not like."

"That sounds an awful lot like a threat." He straightened his arms and then shoved back from the pool table to stand with his hands on his slender hips.

"That's because it is." And I wasn't kidding around this time.

Chapter 6

"My two favorite people!" Mena nearly shouted, breezing into the billiard room in a wave of perfume, smiles, and charisma that pretty much made the walls themselves glow. Mood manipulation to get what she wanted, when she wanted, was her superpower, or at least one of them, and I could feel that she must have supercharged it before entering the room. Had she been standing outside the door, listening to Poobah and me getting into it, and thought she had to come save me?

Because if that was true, then I owed her a huge debt. Maybe she'd settle for a soufflé.

Poobah's frown immediately turned into a smile, and his whole posture softened. When he spread his arms wide, Mena waltzed into them and then shifted so his back was to me. She put one hand around Poobah's back in a half-hug, then draped her other arm around his shoulders and flipped her hand at the wrist over and over, waving me out of the room, mouthing the word "Now." I didn't need to be told twice.

I ducked out of the room as quickly as possible and tried to think where I was going to go next. I didn't want to deal with anyone in my current state. I needed a place to just be by myself and decompress. The library was full of police, Poobah was in the billiard room, and my ladies were in the kitchen. Brushing by the dining room, I saw that the family was still lingering over the food. As far as I was concerned, they could stay there as long as they wanted to.

There was the pavilion out back I could have sat in, but then I might get bombarded by Dean's niece, Amelia. I loved her, I truly did, and every moment spent with her could be an absolute pleasure. But I was not in a good place right now and had way too much on my mind to guard myself against her many questions. Beyond that, she showed some talents I hadn't expected, and I wasn't sure how that would be possible, nor did I know what to do about it. If she did something in my presence that I couldn't explain, I wasn't in the right headspace to process it. At some point, I might have to look into contacting someone within our family who was higher up than me on the hierarchy, but not today.

My room then. I would put myself in my room for a ten-minute timeout and see if I could get my feet back under me.

Heading down the hall, I started making plans. I'd make some lists on who could have done the deed in the library, another of those I should talk to, and one more of possible motives. Maybe I could cross-reference them and then see if Norm was willing to share a few things with me, since he was going to get my help. But if he was going to get info, then I deserved something back to help me.

Same with Poobah. What was it with these men thinking I could do all the heavy lifting, but not meet me halfway?

I plunked myself down on the couch in my room and tried to plan out my next move. It would need to be strategic and maybe a little stealthy. Previously, I had been pretty open about what I was doing when asking questions of people, even if I was a little hidden about what I was also doing with my talent. This might be a gloves-off moment.

Sinking back into the couch, I scoffed at myself. Who did I think I was? Okay, so I'd solved two murders before, and most people believed that the third time was the charm. But did I really think I could do this?

Although I did have my Watson at the ready. Not to mention, my sister could use her talent to help me, as well as finally just telling Glennis that she either told me what I needed to know, or all bets were off.

I started making that list of questions and thoughts, and then someone knocked on my door. Well, it sounded more like they were putting their shoulder into it and banging, not knocking. Who on earth was that?

I opened the door to find myself staring at Earl, our resident ghost. Staring at wasn't exactly the right phrase, since I also could see through him. And through him, I saw that Mena was leaning against the wall in the hallway, as if she had just run some kind of marathon in heels.

I stepped out of my room, grabbed her by the wrist, and yanked her into the sitting room. What had happened? Earl sank into the floor as soon as we crossed the threshold.

After settling her into the couch, I flipped the switch on the tea kettle, then sat next to her, taking her hands into mine.

"Talk to me," I said. "What is wrong with you?"

She straightened right up and gave me one of the smiles that used to make me groan when we were younger. She was up to something, and she had already pulled me in. Now she just needed to tell me which part she had assigned me to.

I had said more than once that she could be exhausting, and I wasn't kidding, but she also could be brilliant in that exhaustion, and right now I had a feeling I was here for it. I probably didn't have a choice, so it made more sense to fall in line instead of trying to fight her.

Still, I closed my eyes and waited for her to lay the plan on me.

"You don't have to do much, just act like this is destroying you, and you want to solve it more than anything else, because Glennis is part of this family, and you have no other goal than to prove she is innocent."

"That's not going to work. I already threatened Poobah."

"Yeah, we're going to have to work on your skills there, Roxy. You can't just run right to the threats. There's an art to getting what you want. I know I taught you better than that."

And that's when I rolled my eyes. "This is not a game, Mena. Someone is dead, and Glennis says she has nothing to do with it. But the woman had Glennis's recipe in her purse, the one Glennis was yelling at me about earlier in the kitchen. And she won't account for where she was during the time of the murder."

"Do you really think Glennis could have done this? Beaning someone in the head with a candlestick in your library? Anywhere in the inn? This place is a second home to her, and she's been here for decades. Killing someone in the house that she considers her own home, outside of the one she lives in down the street, seems ridiculous over a recipe."

I crossed my arms over my chest and frowned. "You didn't see her in the kitchen this morning." I was afraid I sounded pouty and defensive instead of angry or powerful, but I did not care.

"I didn't have to."

"Yes, you would have had to in order to understand. And I noticed that you said she couldn't kill someone *here*, not that she couldn't kill someone *at all*."

She sputtered and stuttered and then sat down on the couch next to me, sinking her head into her hands. "You weren't supposed to catch that part. Why don't my powers work on you?"

I patted her on the shoulder. "They do sometimes, but you were really laying it on thick this time, and I was paying attention."

"Do you really think she did this? That she killed an older woman in the library with a candlestick?"

"That would be awfully *Clue* of her," I said, then sighed. "I don't know, honestly. And I really don't want to believe it, I promise I don't. But I can't rule it out until I can prove it was someone else."

"Then put me to work," Mena said. "Let's get this thing solved and clear Glennis, then we'll go on vacation. And when I get back, we are going to talk to Caper and Dean about Amelia and see if we can't make your happily ever after happen."

I picked at the Afghan on the back of the sofa. "Do you think that's actually going to happen? I'm not sure that I do."

"Don't even start with that. You come from a family of fighters." She frowned at me. "We've played by the rules for a long time, and we've been fine. But we used to break those rules, and we were still just fine. What can they do to us? Shun us? We're pretty insulated as it is and don't really do much outside our family, anyway. They can't take our powers away. And there's every possibility that Amelia is one of us, so we'd be able to tell her family, regardless."

"But what if her family wants her to stop and is horrified by her talents?" It wouldn't have been the first time.

"Are you kidding me? Caper is totally going to try to see if there's a way he could use it to make some money. We're going to have to be very firm about the rules. I'm willing to go against the uppers about love, but not about crime-type stuff. I might talk some people into things they might not have wanted to do at first, but it's never anything that will hurt them or put them in danger."

"Well, there was that one incident..."

She pinched me, and I laughed for the first time in what felt like hours.

"How am I going to get Poobah to tell me what Glennis has on him or what he has on her?" I grabbed a pillow and tucked it against my stomach. "It's so frustrating that he keeps putting me off. She works for me, and I feel like I should know if there's something that she knows that would make us vulnerable if it came out."

"I could try to talk with her." With a shrug, she sank back into the couch. "My powers don't always work on her outside of making sure she cuts my pieces of cake bigger than anyone else's, but it might be worth a try, if you're okay with that?"

"Absolutely. In fact, why don't you go start now?" I had just watched Dean walk past my window, and I found myself very much needing to be in his presence. He made me feel calmer, and things always seemed to make more sense when he was around. That scared me, too. No matter how much I wanted to trust it, I was a little afraid. I had never really expected to find anyone to spend my life with unless they just happened to work at the inn for the duration. This place was my life and the only dream I'd wanted. Dean butting in was very welcome, but also very different from what I had thought life would be. And I was trying to transition into living in the now, instead of hanging onto the life I thought I'd have, instead of enjoying the one I did have.

It might not be easy, but I sure was going to try. And trying meant going after Dean out in the backyard, and then dragging him into the house so that we could start going through what we knew, what we didn't know, and how we might make those two meet in the middle.

I stepped outside the door from the kitchen as he turned toward the small cottage in the back. I'd opened it up for his brother, niece, and nephew to live in while they were getting things back in line after some trouble. If Dean was here for them, I didn't want to infringe on their time.

But it was as if he sensed me. After half a second, he stopped and pivoted on the toe of his work boot. When he finally faced me, his smile was spread wide, and so were his arms. I wanted to run to him, perhaps with some swelling background music. Instead, I forced myself to walk, but did not stop myself from wrapping my arms around his waist and then resting my head on his chest and just feeling his heartbeat in his muscular chest.

"What happened?" He stroked my short hair, and I sighed.

"Poobah beat me at pool, then told me that he's been spending all his time expanding his skills because he has nothing else to do in his retirement. Then he said my grandmother often cheated with War. And he wants me to look into who killed Penny because I need to clear Glennis, but she won't tell me where she was, and he won't tell me what she has over him that makes him give her so much leeway."

"I've only been gone for like an hour."

"Sixty-three minutes and it's been intense." I nestled my cheek more firmly onto his chest.

"What about your sister?"

"She's willing to help." But I couldn't tell him how she was going to help, not in full. And I couldn't tell him that I would also get the rubbings from the pool table that showed what kind of plans my relatives had put together centuries ago about our talents. I hated this. I hated not being able to talk to the person I considered my best friend and my partner-in-life things. But my talent made it so that I could only share half of myself, and that sucked. Maybe we'd have to step up looking into Ameila and her talent. I didn't want to fast-track it and hurt Amelia just to get what I wanted, but the temptation was definitely there.

He kissed the top of my hair. "Would you believe me if I told you it was all going to be okay, and I've asked Isaac to do some online research. He's got those fast fingers, and he's bored until school starts. He tried some online gaming, but apparently that's beneath him at this point."

I chuckled, and he gave me a squeeze.

"It'll be good for him, and maybe he can use it later on, after he graduates. You piqued his interest last time, so now he's talking about being a private investigator. Caper isn't exactly happy about that, but he'll probably figure out a way to use it to his advantage."

That made me think about Mena saying that we could help Amelia, but only if Caper would not use her powers to his gain. So many things in so many different directions. But first and foremost, we needed to find the killer.

"Do you have plans tonight?" I asked.

"I was having dinner with these clowns over here before everyone left. Caper has decided to take the kids out to Jim Thorpe to do some railroad stuff."

"So, it really is going to be just you and me here?"

"Yep." I could hear the smile in his voice.

"I might get spoiled." I tipped my head back and grinned at him.

"No might about it. But first..."

"Yeah, all right, get Isaac on things, and have dinner with your family, and then we'll get back together tomorrow."

"You could join us. I'm sure everyone would love that."

"I appreciate that, but I have some of my own stuff to do." Like, hopefully contacting Earl the house ghost and seeing if he had anything to add. And get with Mena to see what she'd learned. And see if I could needle Poobah into telling me anything about Glennis to help me solve the mystery instead of adding to it.

Ohhhh...And perhaps see if I could find anything in Penny's room. I was the innkeeper, after all, which meant I had the keys to every room in my castle. I assumed that Norm had already checked things over there, but I'd found things he hadn't before, and that might work again. It was worth a try. So, I put that on my mental list. Along with getting into the library and finding that sparkly book from earlier. "Lots to do, especially since the family is staying overnight again. Norm said that they can't go home, so I offered a free night for everyone."

"Isn't that going to cost you? I'm sure they have the money to pay."

"I'm sure they do, too, but this is the right thing to do, and they appreciated it. Well, everyone except that Leon guy, who was trying to leave earlier this morning, until his wife told him that he had promised to give her the week without his super important businessman stuff schtick."

He hummed in his throat. "Maybe he has something to do with this, and Penny was already dead, and he wanted to get out before anyone found her." He looked off into the distance. "Maybe that was his plan all along."

"My Watson." I snuggled back in and then added that to my mental list, too.

"My Sherlock better get to work then, and see what he's got going for him. I'll talk to Isaac to see if he's found anything. I can shoot it to you through text if that's okay?"

"Absolutely." I smiled up at him. "I will wait breathlessly for any info." And then I laughed when he kissed me on the nose.

"Aw, but ew," Amelia said, emerging from the small cottage at the back of my property. I had considered for some time making it into a small house for myself so that I could be close, but not actually in the inn itself. But when Dean's extended family's situation came to my attention, I put that desire aside and opened it up to them. Best decision I'd made in a long time. Well, except for taking a chance with the man who was currently sticking his tongue out at his niece.

"Rude," she said, but then stuck her tongue out at him, too.

"Children, you're both being rude." Caper stood in the doorway of the cottage, leaning nonchalantly on the door frame that he'd repainted a few months ago. He'd done a lot to spruce up the small abode, and I appreciated it.

We hadn't spoken about how much it cost to live here, or even what I expected from him. I'd just told them to move in, and we'd figure stuff out later. And I hadn't decided on when later was just yet.

Some of that had to do with knowing he was finding his footing after being in some trouble with the law, but also knowing that he had two kids who thought the world of him, even as I also knew they were honest with what he had done before to survive. Being a thief was not exactly on my resume, and he said he had only taken on people who were bad and should be put in their place. But I was hoping he'd take this opportunity to get things right, like he had before he'd fallen off the better path for the kids. And he seemed to be doing well, while also fixing the cottage. Win-win, as far as I was concerned.

"Are those flowers I see in the window boxes?" I asked, finally looking past Dean's chest to really take in what had changed about this little place. I could see it from the inn, but hadn't really been this close in a few weeks. Everyone here seemed to come into the inn at one point or another: Amelia to study in the library, Isaac to talk Glennis out of all kinds of treats, and Caper to help Dean fix things here or there as needed.

Sometimes Amelia also came in to use the phone booth under the stairs, but I didn't say anything about that since she was safe, and I wasn't sure who she had told.

Speaking of Amelia, she kept jerking her head over toward the gazebo to the right. We'd had a pretty intense talk there a few months ago during the last murder investigation. She hadn't said much about seeing lights or recognizing ghosts since then, and I'd left it alone. I wondered, though, if that was about to come back up.

I wasn't ready. What would I say? I wasn't the one who did these kinds of things. Heck, I barely understood my own talent. If she had questions, I'd probably lead her the wrong way, no matter what I said.

But I couldn't escape her. Dean gave me one last kiss that was far too short, but very sweet, and then went in the front door behind Caper. Isaac swung out at the last second to wave at me and give me a thumbs up, then faded back into the house.

Amelia, though, didn't take the same cue and walk back into the house. Instead, she followed me and then grabbed my elbow and pulled me into the gazebo before I could shuffle my way past it fast enough.

"I think I might have done something I wasn't supposed to," she said, her eyes bright with tears, and her hands clasped in front of her small chest.

Uh-oh.

Chapter 7

How bad was something bad from a twelve-year-old? Sometimes their idea of bad was my idea of mildly not awesome, so I wanted to step carefully here. Although I was dealing with Amelia, who happened to have seen far more in her short life than most people had to deal with over the course of decades, if ever.

To be honest, I needed backup for this and more info from people like Aunt Hellen or Uncle Vince, who were actual trainers. What if I led her wrong? Or what if she had done something I couldn't explain and wasn't able to keep her from making the mistake worse?

Over the last few months, she had shown some signs of being able to use magic in the form of aeromancy. It was the ability to use the atmosphere and natural surroundings to channel magic. I'd done some research in our archives on what that meant exactly, and we appeared not to have had one in about a hundred years, so I didn't have anyone to talk to with actual experience. Uncle Vince was supposed to know about all talents, and even he had been kind of stumped as to what she might be able to do and how to do it. He'd put out feelers to others months ago, but we still hadn't heard anything from them.

It was time to ask again and not let this drag out. I knew that part of me loved the idea of her having powers, which then would make it possible to bring all of her family into the fold with my family. If that happened, I could truly be my whole self with the man I loved. But there was a part of me that was incredibly afraid he would be so taken aback about the whole magic thing that they'd shield Amelia from us, take her away, deny what she could do, and leave us all forever.

My stomach churned just thinking about it.

I refocused on Amelia, though, because she didn't know what was going on in my head, and I'd waited too long to answer her. "I'm sure it's okay. What do you think you did?"

"I don't know, but it has to do with the phone under the stairs." She looked away and then back, with glassy eyes.

"That old thing? I don't think there's anything wrong with using that to play if you want to." I shrugged to show that I really wasn't that concerned.

"But someone answered."

"Was it a guy?" My brain started kicking on, but I let it subside from the anxiety. Earl, our resident ghost, was the only one who used that thing, and he was safe. No one had even remembered the phone booth was there under the stairs until it had started ringing a few months ago to help with the last murder investigation. Earl was relatively harmless and, in fact, had helped a lot. If he'd answered her continuous calls once, then I was not going to fret about things.

"I think so! Do you know who it was? I just pushed some random numbers, and suddenly he was on the other side of the line asking if I was okay."

"I don't know exactly who it was." A little bit of a lie, but one I was willing to tell. I knew some of Earl's backstory and who he was today, but I didn't know everything. Which led me to caution her. "Let's not go in the phone booth for the next little while, at least until I can talk to Poobah about how someone could have answered a random call. I think that might be safer. It was okay when it was just you pressing numbers, but if it's a line out to another phone, then I need to look into that before we do anything else. Deal?"

She nodded, biting her lip.

"Promise? I really need you to be careful, Amelia. I know you love it here, and I love it here for you. But something happened today, and I'm going to be looking into it, so I don't want to also have to come looking for you." I put an arm around her shoulders, and she leaned in on the gazebo bench, putting her head on my chest. This child was an entire world unto herself, and I adored her. I only hoped I could continue to adore her on the property, instead of from afar, if Dean decided that it was unsafe here with the paranormal, that we were unsafe.

She blew out a breath. "Yeah, I promise. But only if you'll let me know as soon as I can go in the phone booth again. There's something about it that makes me feel settled, even when things aren't always going right around here."

That stopped me in my tracks, but I did everything I could not to tense up. "What's been going wrong around here lately? Anything I can help with?" Anything horrendous was what I really wanted to ask, but I had to tread lightly here, too, so as not to scare her away.

"Just Isaac. He's decided that he's too old to have anything to do with me. Dad had warned me that the time might come for this, but I guess I just wasn't ready." There was that shrug again, and my heart hurt for her. Even if she didn't want me to step in and help, I was definitely going to be talking to Dean so he could talk to the kid. Since Amelia and Isaac were both homeschooled, they didn't really know anyone outside of their family, and their family had to stick together.

Although…an idea was surfacing in my head, one I might just run with. I could possibly lean on some of the families around town about having a little shindig at the inn to see if Amelia would connect with some of the people her age around here. We had a lot of good people, and if Caper and his family were staying, which they appeared to be, then it might be time to introduce them around town.

But not until after I figured out who had killed Penny in the library with the candlestick.

I kissed Amelia on the head and felt her smile against my collarbone. "We'll figure it out, but please stay away from the phone booth for right now. I promise to let you know the second it's cleared."

"Okay," she said and threw her arms around my neck. "Thank you for everything. I've never felt so safe or at home, and I just wanted to thank you for that. Even if it doesn't last, at least I knew what it felt like for a little while." Her words were muffled because they were said into my shoulder, but I felt each one like a punch in the gut.

And then she jumped up from the bench and ran to the house without looking back.

What if, in teasing out her talent and talking to Caper and Dean about it, I inadvertently ripped her away from the only home she'd ever felt was hers? There was that sick-to-the-stomach feeling again. Lots of people had no idea they had talent. Maybe it just showed up as being better at something without much practice or effort. Maybe it just seemed to come to them naturally that they could read the stars, or talk to the trees and be answered on the breeze. Just something a little special that they took as a neat trick, but nothing to actually look at as a real talent.

And they survived. Our heritage, and the umbrella we all lived under, had cracked a few times throughout the centuries, and some of the tree branches had fallen off here and there. It was impossible to know everyone who had those talents, only those who had stayed within the fold. Maybe it was time to start patching up the umbrella.

But again, not now. I had a murder to solve. And when I glanced over at the windows that showed the library from floor to ceiling in all its glory, I could see that the police were finally leaving with all their kits in their hands. Hopefully, they'd found something, so I didn't have to do a deep dive into Glennis and every other person in the establishment. But until I knew who had done this, I was on the case. And that meant going after the book that had sparkled earlier in the library and hopefully getting some fireworks and a direction to look in.

As quickly as I could, I jumped up from the bench myself and hustled to the back door into the kitchen, hoping to catch those police before they left the inn. No harm in trying to see if they'd share anything they'd found, if they'd found anything, so I could have that info. Norm had conceded that he might need my help, but that didn't mean he was also going to help me.

But I would force them to say no this time instead of just hoping that they would look at me as assisting, as opposed to being a pain. I saw the back of Micah as the front door started swinging closed. I could tell by his red hair. Should I shout out his name?

Aunt Hellen took that choice right out of my hands. "Micah! A minute of your time, please?" She flicked her gaze over to me, and I stepped back around the corner, so I could hear what they said, but not be seen. I trusted that Aunt Hellen would ask the right questions. Heck, they'd probably be better and more pointed than I would have felt comfortable asking.

There was a mirror in the hallway with me that allowed me to see into the lobby, but not have anyone in the lobby see me. Perfection.

Micah held the door open with one hand and bent his head. His shoulders slumped like he knew what he was about to get himself into, but he probably figured it would be better to do it now than to make her chase him down into the circular driveway out front.

She waited at the front counter with her hands folded in front of the keyboard. As if she had all the time in the world, while he turned around, closed the door, and looked longingly over his shoulder as he watched everyone else load up their cars.

"What can I do for you, ma'am?"

I ducked back further into the hallway as he approached the desk, making sure I would not be seen.

"You're a good boy, Micah, and I appreciate your level head in the middle of this craziness we seem to be experiencing lately."

His face flamed a little red, and a small smile peeked out on his face. He shut that down really fast and shook his head. "Flattery is not going to help you here, Hellen."

"That's not flattery. I'm not very good at running around the subject. I was trying, but since you don't seem to want to ease into anything, I'm just going to go right into what you should be doing."

Sticking a hand on his hip, he dropped his chin. I was pretty sure he was just now realizing that he had shot himself in the foot. This could have been easier, maybe softer, but he was the one who decided to go the other direction.

"Let's get right into it then. Norm got his ass handed to him over the last two murder investigations, from what I've heard, and now he wants to see if Roxy can help him. But you and I both know he is not going to reciprocate on that, and honestly, that is completely unacceptable. I'm not going to confront Norm on that because it will do nothing but piss him off, but I'm going to tell you right now that anything you have that can help her should be shared immediately. If you want help, then you have to also help, or I'm going to tell Roxy to keep her nose out of it, and you all can swing on your own."

They stared at each other for a full minute until Mena came waltzing into the middle of things with that smile. Did she know when this kind of thing was happening? Like, did it ping in her brain that something was going on, and she followed it like a trail to chaos? Did she also have sparkles that signaled when things were happening that she needed to pay attention to? I'd have to ask, but not now, since I was supposed to be in hiding and not even here.

"Oh, good, Micah, you're still here! I wanted to see if you were interested in some tortellini that Glennis is trying out for dinner tonight, since we're going to have guests longer than we had anticipated. You like tortellini, don't you? Who doesn't?"

He flamed red again, and then the half smile popped again, but this time he didn't try to stop it. He toed the carpet in front of him. If he clasped his hands in front of him and started swaying like an elementary school boy who just had his crush see him for the first time, I was not going to be able to keep myself from puking a little. But I told myself to stop it. If it got me what I wanted, then I had to take what I could get, and however I could get it.

"I do like tortellini."

"Of course, you do!" She playfully patted him on the shoulder, then let her fingers linger on his biceps. "Working out?"

The faint blush on his face brightened to a shade of red usually only found in crayon boxes.

Mena plowed on. "Well, she'd love to make it for you. I was wondering, though, if you could get a quick picture of the recipe card, back and front, because I guess it's a big recipe, and then you can come to the kitchen and do some taste testing. Can you do that for me, Micah? Please? It would mean the world and really help."

"Sure. Of course."

"Come back later, and I'll give you my cell number to text it to me. Okay? Have we got a deal?" she asked.

"We sure do, Mena. See you soon." And he trotted out the door, with a bit of a skip in his step, then headed to his car in the drive.

"You can come out now," Mena said.

"Okay, Glinda the Good Witch." I strode out around the corner into the hallway. "How long does the thrall work on people? Since it usually doesn't work on me, I'm curious to know if he'll actually follow through, or if he'll forget, or realize that he promised something he can't actually deliver on as soon as you're no longer in his sights."

She frowned at me. "You know, sometimes I'm just being nice and asking for something that someone already wants to do, but needs a certain form of permission to do it. It's not always magic, Roxy."

There was a snort to my left.

"Aunty Hell!" Mena turned with her hands stuck on her hips and scowled.

"Darling, I love you like almost no one else could, and even I'm wondering if you're lying to yourself."

"I am not, and even if I were, we need that recipe. If getting it will make Glennis stop fretting in the kitchen, she'd be happy to make tortellini. She might not have the actual card, but from what she was telling me, it's the information on it that she needs more than the physical item. I don't know what for, but she ruined my whole getting ice cream experience by whipping up so much negative energy in the kitchen I left before she could sour the milk used from our favorite creamery."

Now, who was being dramatic?

"Fine," I said. "But as soon as he gets that to you, I want it texted to me, not Glennis. I need to see what it says before we release it to her, or I'll never get any answers from her or Poobah."

"What answers are you looking for, dear?" Aunt Hellen asked. Funny how Mena got to be darling, and I was just dear. I made her life easy. I should have been the darling, but that was an issue for another time.

"First off, I want to know what Glennis has on Poobah that she's allowed to do whatever she wants, with no thought to professionalism, and just assumes that he'll make things okay for her. Second, I want to know what is on that freaking card that's important enough that I have some real concerns that, even if Glennis didn't kill Penny, that she might have if she'd known the woman had the recipe card. And third, why did Penny have the card in the first place? What is the significance of this thing? And those are just the ones I have about a card." I bounced my gaze back and forth between the two women when no one said anything. "I'll be in the library if you need me. Mena, do not give that card to Glennis until I see it. Promise me." I might not have had her talent of getting promises people didn't want to make, but I did have the upper hand as the older sister, and she knew better than to lie to me.

"Absolutely, just as soon as I look it over myself and see what I might be able to glean from it."

I sighed because that was the best I was going to get. "Let me know the second Micah comes back. I'll hide in the hallway again if I have to, but I want to know as soon as he sets foot on the property."

Mena folded her lips in and slowly blinked. Was that a tell? Could she track people knowing what they were up to if she'd set them on a mission with their promises? Another question, and that meant we were going to have to have a real sit-down and discussion about what she could do, and how she could do it, if I wanted her to remain on the property.

I squinted at her. "For some reason, I think you know more about a lot of things than you're letting on. We'll discuss that after the library. Don't go running away until we do."

"Fine."

I glanced one more time at Aunt Hellen. "Anything you want to add to this amazing conversation before I take myself off to the books?"

"Just wondering what we're going to do with all these people when we thought they'd be gone today. They seem to have all dispersed to their rooms, but I don't think they're going to stay there forever. We might want to actually put Glennis on those tortellini, or something similar, in order to be ready when the brunch they devoured wears off."

"I'll leave that in your capable hands. Glennis doesn't really want to talk to me just now, and I'm afraid I might demand something that will make her walk. Keep it easy and low cost, if possible. I'm willing to take the hit for tonight, but if I don't solve this soon, we might have to talk about the upcoming days and how I can keep them here, without going bankrupt."

With that, I took myself off down the hallway in search of that sparkly book in the library. It had better deliver, because with the mood I was currently in, I had no idea if my tolerance would take anything less than full obedience at this point.

At least that's the way I started out, stalking down the hallway, like a soldier set on a mission of do or die. But with each step, I felt my ire subsiding a little. Yes, I wanted the killer found. Yes, I wanted to know what was going on. Yes, I also wanted to know how bound Poobah and Glennis were, and what that steel string was all about. But I also wanted peace here, and was this really worth upsetting my entire world?

Maybe, maybe not. I wouldn't know until I was in the middle of it and figuring out the very real whodunnit that had been placed, yet again, at my inn.

With that thought, I pushed open the door to the library and stood at the threshold for a moment to center myself. I needed to be clear on my intentions here and ask for exactly what I wanted. It didn't always work, but it definitely wouldn't work if I went in all willy-nilly.

As soon as I crossed onto the floor, the sparkles lit up in the far corner. I quickly closed the door behind me and locked it. I wanted full privacy. I wished I could also close off the floor-to-ceiling windows on the other side of the room, but there were no curtains. I would just have to make sure my back was turned whenever I did something. As far as I knew, no one who didn't have a talent could see the sparkles, and even those who did have the talent saw them differently, so I had hope that I was relatively safe in here.

It didn't smell like death as I walked by the chair where I had found Penny slumped over. But I could feel the pall in the air and knew I was going to have to come in here and do some kind of cleansing ritual before the day was over. I wasn't worried that her spirit had lingered, so much as I was concerned the aura of death would remain.

I put that aside and followed the trail of sparkles that grew more vibrant with every step. The book was calling to me, and I only hoped that it understood that I was here for answers, not more riddles that I couldn't figure out.

Chapter 8

The showers of sparkles, coming from the bookshelf in the far corner, were almost blinding the closer I got. Because the book resided on the shelf behind a glass insert, I loved seeing the light show, but this was a little much. Did it mean something that it was throwing off sparks like a bonfire gone crazy?

I was about to find out.

Using the key on a chain at my waist, I unlocked the cabinet and then slid the glass front up into the track above the shelf. The tome was a massive book of fairy tales from Scotland, a place that I knew some of my line came from years ago. I dragged it out, almost dropping it on the ground because of its dimensions and the weight it carried with all the thicker than normal pages. It had been made over three centuries ago and had been a rare find for Poobah when he'd taken one of his few vacations by himself. He'd come back full of glee with the book in his hand and had been absolutely delighted to make me close my eyes and hold out my hands for the "souvenir" he'd bought me, since he hadn't taken me with him.

I'd nearly dropped the book then, too, not expecting the weight of it when he placed it on my upturned palms. I'd felt a warmth before I'd been allowed to open my eyes, and something had zinged up my arm. At the time, I had just thought it was amazing when I'd opened my eyes as quickly as he'd told me I could. All other thoughts went out of my head as I turned to place the book on a hand-carved lectern from the local college and reverently used one fingertip to open the front cover.

The beautifully scripted type, set by some printer long, long ago, was accentuated by lovely paintings showing the different characters that populated common fairy tales, as well as those that few who hadn't looked into the lore knew about.

I had never gotten any messages from this book, though I'd tried. Why now?

However, it really didn't matter why now, as long as it gave me something to work with that I could use. And no more riddles.

Closing my eyes, I stepped out of my sensible kitten heels and grounded myself to the floor by sinking my toes into the carpet. I drew in a deep breath and then released it as I rested my right palm on the elaborate cover of the book. I was ready. "Help me find the killer of Penny. Where do I need to look first?"

I stuck my index finger in between the pages of the book, feeling the smooth paper along my fingertip, and then flipped the thing open. And for the third time, I almost dropped it, as a full-on fireworks show began from the second I started cracking open the book. Sparks shot out, erupting in a multitude of colors. That was new.

The show was great, of course, but I needed it to tell me something.

The room is the key as well as the teddy.

What in the freaking heck did that mean?

The light show died. The sparkly letters that had risen from the aged pages sank back into the black ink.

"I need more! What else can I do? What room? What key? What does it mean by a teddy?" I barely stopped myself from slamming the book onto the lectern. Instead, I took a deep breath and gently set the book on the desk to my left, then placed my hand on it. I needed paper. Thankfully, I found it in the drawer of the desk. I kept all of the furniture in here stocked with paper and pens, just in case anyone would need to write something down. I was that someone, at this point, and I was all too pleased with myself.

"The room is the key and the teddy." I tapped the pen to my chin. "No, the room is the key, as well as the teddy. Okay, I asked for guidance, I got guidance, even if it's a little vague. I can work with this. I can't tell Dean, though. Damn."

But I did think about what room the book could be referencing. And then it hit me. Penny's room. I assumed that the police had looked in there, but previously, when we'd had a murder here, I had still found things in there that the police had not.

Quickly replacing the book in the case, I steadied my hands and took another one of those deep breaths. I could do this. I could couch it as looking into Penny's room to Dean without having to explain why, or how I came to the conclusion that we should look. And I could take a gander all on my own first, since he was spending time with his family, and I had some time before we had to do the dinner thing.

After locking the case, I hovered my hand in front of the glass, not touching it, because I didn't want to have to clean my fingerprints or smudges, if possible. Please, let this be the answer that would get me started on the right path to finding Penny's killer.

Grabbing the piece of paper with the words on it, I tried to think of what the teddy might be. Please, don't let it be a piece of clothing...

I remembered at the last second to unlock the main door to the library before dragging it toward me, thankfully. And then I was off and doing my own trotting. Hopefully, no one would see me skipping in my heels that I had also remembered to slip my feet back into right before I left.

I decided to take the back stairs to the second floor instead of walking past Aunt Hellen. Maybe I could take a second, too, and sweet-talk Glennis into telling me what I needed to know about her whereabouts and what was so freaking important about the recipe card. I didn't have Mena's talent, but maybe if I put more effort into not needling Glennis, and instead, just took her at face value, that would work in my favor.

I slowed my roll and walked calmly into the kitchen. Skipping would be frowned upon, not to mention my toes were starting to hurt from the pressure of each impact. As soon as I saw that there was no one in here doing the busy work, I was incredibly deflated.

I was so used to seeing her bustle around in here, humming to herself or talking to the utensils and herbs, telling them to help her out. I didn't want to not have that anymore. Yes, I wanted to know what she had on Poobah. Admittedly, I also wanted to sort out why she often felt combative with me when I was the owner. I loved having her here, but I wanted less pushback. I was so wrapped up in my thoughts that I didn't realize at first that she actually was in the room with me. Huddled in the corner on a stool with her face in her hands.

"Glennis?" I said softly. If she had been anyone else, I would have placed a gentle hand on her hunched shoulder, hoping I could help in some way. Instead, I stood back and just softly called her name again. "Glennis?"

"I'll have dinner ready on time," she said, lifting her head and straightening her shoulders. "Don't worry about me. I'm capable of multi-tasking."

"I'm very aware of that. You're the best multitasker I've ever met, to be completely honest. I could never run a kitchen like you do."

"And I could never run the inn like you do. We both have our talents."

The use of that word took me a step back in my head, but I held my ground. Was that what it was? Had Poobah slipped up in front of her once and shown her his talent? Was that what she had over him? That if he didn't let her do and say whatever she wanted, she would out our family as witches?

I didn't have time to contemplate that too much, though, because she was still talking.

"I'm sorry about how I handled this morning, and all the things I am refusing to do. I have reasons, I promise, and I'm trying to figure out how to work around things I don't want to talk about. Honestly, things I don't even want to think about. I know that's very vague, and I'm actually very sorry about that, but there's too much in my head to make sense of it all right now. I'm trying, though. I promise, I am trying."

Tears glistened in her eyes, and my heart thudded in my chest. I'd never seen Glennis cry. Never. She was bluster, catty, and full of sass. Not tears!

What was I supposed to do now?

I followed my gut as much as I could. "It's okay, Glennis. We'll figure it out. But if there's anything that you can tell me, or anything that you can share, it would really help me and your nephew, so we can get the real killer behind bars."

She gave a slight nod, and I waited for her to maybe say something, but nothing more came of it.

I sighed. I had so hoped for more, but maybe it was just too soon. I'd check in with her later. For now, I needed to get up to Penny's room. Hopefully, it was the room the book had talked about.

"I'm heading upstairs to check on some stuff. Do you need anything?" It was an open-ended question, and I'd admit that I was hoping it would be an invitation for her to maybe offer something. No one could ever say I gave up easily.

"No, I heard I'm supposed to make some tortellini. I have it in the fridge, thawing from the last time I made way too much. I'll make sure to have a good sauce and some bread. Do you want a salad, too? I'll have to run to the grocery store to get the makings, since I thought we were done this morning. I hadn't ordered anything that couldn't be saved until we all get back from vacation."

"Totally understandable, and a salad would be great. Put anything on the account at the store, and I'll handle settling up with Mr. Grant."

She stood and removed her apron, this time much more gently than this morning. How was that less than ten hours ago?

"I'll be back. Do you want me to lock the kitchen?"

"No, I'll get it when I come back down. I don't think anyone has been out of their rooms since they finished brunch. Everyone seems to be taking time to grieve, so let's just respect that and go from there. Text me if you need anything. I have my phone on me." I mainly had it on me, waiting to hear that Mena had come through with the pictures, but I hadn't heard anything from her yet. What was the holdup?

"I'll be back then." She removed her purse from under the counter and shuffled out of the kitchen. Her whole body looked slumped and defeated, and I wondered what exactly was weighing so heavily on her and why I couldn't get her to talk to me. Admittedly, we were not always on the same wavelength, but we did have a relatively good relationship, and she'd been in my life since day one.

I watched her walk out, then heard her say goodbye to Aunt Hellen. Time to get this show on the road upstairs.

Opening the door situated at the back of the kitchen, I mounted the stairs that had originally been built for servants. I was the only one who normally used them. Everyone else just used the normal stairs. But I liked these, and it would let me out from behind a floor-to-ceiling painting at the top of the landing.

I would also be right across from Penny's room, and I had the keys in my pocket to let me into the room just in case it was locked. Eventually, I'd need to ask Micah if they had gone over the room, or if they hadn't yet gotten to that, since they'd spent so much time in the library, dusting for clues and picking up evidence.

Turning the knob on the door, I was a little nervous that it turned freely. Which meant it wasn't locked, and anyone and everyone could have gone in and out of here. Was the scene still intact? Had anyone, like Leon or Jessica, gone in and rifled through things to get any information that they wanted?

Leon, because in his conversation with his wife this morning, had said they outnumbered Penny. Outnumbered her for what? And Jessica, because she was convinced Penny's memoir had been destroyed. But was that actually true? I was incredibly interested in whatever event Jessica thought should never have happened and didn't need to be talked about.

I had a bit of a list going in my head and would need to write it all down, but first I had to look around the room.

It was pristine when I entered. The bed was perfectly made, as if it had not been slept in last night. The drawers were all tucked in, as they should be. The armchair in the corner, next to the window, was perfectly positioned with its small, embroidered pillow just waiting to be leaned on. Even the carpet looked like it had barely been trodden on. Normally, the pile was shuffled one way or another, depending on how people chose to walk throughout the room. But there were still vacuum tracks visible where the maids would have cleaned it last week before the family had gotten here. How was that possible?

Well, there were some foot tracks or shoe imprints when I looked a little closer. But I didn't remember Penny having big feet, and these tracks were made with big feet. Could it have been one of the police officers? Maybe I'd ask Mena to ask Micah. That could get complicated if I kept having to go through a third party, but if it got me the answers I was looking for, then I didn't think I had much choice.

So, if this was the room, and it was the key, according to the book, then what was I looking for? And again, I was begging for it not to be a teddy, as in lingerie that she would have worn for one reason or another. I was all about you being you, and if negligees were your thing, then have at it. I just didn't want to have to touch them and then hand them over to the police with little to no explanation as to why I thought it might be significant.

Carefully closing the door behind me, I set my phone on the tall chest of drawers and began looking around. We'd have to pack everything that was in the dresser and closet, if it wasn't already done. And I'd make sure to clear it with the cops before I sent it home with one of the family members. But before I did that, I wanted to spy around to see what could make this room the key and where a teddy fit into the whole thing.

I spent about fifteen minutes opening every drawer and cabinet, looking under the bed and the mattress, checking behind curtains and on shelves, even the ones I had to climb onto a chair to make sure there was nothing hidden up there.

And after those fifteen minutes were over, I found nothing. At this point, I would have welcomed a teddy, even if it had been a piece of clothing, just to not feel like I hadn't wasted all that time. But I found nothing, and that was more than disappointing. It was irritating. How was I supposed to solve this, and why was I asking a book if it wasn't going to help? And even when it did, it was too vague to understand what was going on. Ugh.

Letting myself out of the room, I turned to lock the door when someone cleared their throat behind me. I wanted to jump, but I clamped down on that urge before I did it. I had every right to be in the room, and no need to explain myself.

I turned around and found myself face-to-chest with Leon.

"I need to get into the room," he said, his arms crossed over his chest and his chin jutted out.

"I'm sorry, but that's not going to be possible at this time. I've been asked to keep it locked up tight until further investigation can be done." Not a lie because I didn't say it was the police who had asked for that, or what the investigation could mean.

"We have valuables in there that I must have back."

I nodded briefly. "Of course, and I'm sure you'll get them back, just as soon as things are solved." Again, not a lie, and I'd happily hand over a piece of Penny's belongings, just as soon as I knew who had killed her, and what a teddy had to do with it.

He scoffed at me, but he did take a step back, and I didn't have to crane my neck so hard to be able to meet his gaze. I was not backing down here.

"Dinner should be ready about seven, since the brunch was so much later in the day. Maybe after that you can get what you're looking for."

"Do the police not think it was a natural death?" he asked. "Why do they need access to her belongings and rooms if she simply suffered a heart attack. Her doctor has been telling her that's what would happen over the last decade, and she never took it seriously. The woman was still running around with different men every week and dancing until she was out of breath, but heaven forbid she eat anything that wasn't fried or breaded."

It was important to be careful here, so I said as little as possible. "I'm not certain what they want, or why they want it. I only know that the room might be important, and so I have to keep it closed and locked, until further notice."

He groaned and turned on his heel, but then he turned back. "If they really want to get the dirt on Penny, they'll want to look at your other guest who left much earlier this morning, right when I wanted to leave. That Walter guy wasn't here by accident, no matter how the family refuses to acknowledge it." He stomped off with his hands jammed into his hips and yelled for Sally.

Now wasn't that intriguing?

Chapter 9

As soon as Sally whipped open the door to their room down the hall and demanded Leon be quiet, I left my post. I triple checked the lock, then pocketed the key. No one was getting in there without my permission again. I took the front stairs down to the desk, where I hoped Aunt Hellen was not working at the moment, so I could look into the computer without having to explain myself when I really didn't know what I was looking for in the first place.

Did the family know that Penny had been murdered now? I thought they had been left in the dark, but I had no way of asking without showing my own hand. I did not want to be the one who told them if Leon was just guessing.

Who was Walter, though? I hadn't seen him do anything with the family. In fact, I'd barely seen him at all during his short stay. He'd called to see if there was room for him to do some painting. According to him, he was in desperate need of finishing up a gallery spread two towns over in two weeks. We'd had the room available, so I'd given it to him, especially because it was on the third floor, away from everyone else. He was more than fine with that and had also said he hadn't wanted any food either.

So, was that my guy? There seemed to be quite a few people who might have had it out for Penny, but why this one?

I thought she had been a very nice person. Often, she seemed to be thinking about her family and had even paid for every single one of them to be here for a week that was supposed to be all about the family. Had I misunderstood or completely been ignorant in thinking things had gone well when really they had been far more angsty than I'd realized? Normally, I was very keyed into this kind of thing. Now I wondered if, in my glee for having Dean at my side, and leaving a lot of things to the rest of the staff, I'd unplugged myself from my normal awareness of the situation and the people who were staying here.

I wouldn't lie, I wasn't a fan of that particular theory, but I wasn't going to let it stop me from looking into this as much as I had to.

What did I need to know, though? And what did I actually think was going to be in our reservation system? It wasn't like we did a background check on every guest. Although with the mysteries that had come into our area over the last several months, I might rethink that.

For now, I walked down the last few stairs to the front desk and was relieved to see Aunt Hellen gone. She should have been at the desk, and on any other day, I would have wondered where she might be and what she might be doing. But right now, I was just thankful that the space was open so I could do a little sleuthing myself without anyone watching over my shoulder. Before I got started, though, I left a note for her to make sure we told the cleaning staff to catch up with the dusting. I'd been meaning to do that ever since I'd been in the library. Plus, with the mess the police had made in there, it was due for a good going over.

Now, on to the searching. Waking the computer up, I waited for it to cycle through whatever it had to, and then as soon as I typed in my password and opened the desktop, I dug into Walter.

Walter Blenden had checked in late at night on the same day as the family. There was a note on his reservation that he had called from the car to see if we had anything available. He'd been referred by the writing group we had every year for a conference. Aunt Hellen had given him the last room, and we'd charged his credit card with no problems.

So far, so good.

I wasn't the best at doing any kind of research on people, since that was not really part of my job description. As long as you paid your bill and didn't wreck anything in my establishment, I didn't need to know much more than that about you. But I was going to have to dig in here.

With that in mind, I put his name into a search bar on the internet. A few images popped up, but I couldn't tell if it was the same person, because he was much older now than in any of the pictures online. There were also a few paintings in the images, a small gallery showing here and there. They were pretty, even if they wouldn't have been something I'd buy for the inn. I leaned more toward landscapes with water involved and darker pictures with weather present. His were often of animals and cityscapes. To each his own.

I made a few notes. Perhaps if I gave them to Isaac, he could see if he could find anything more in his web mastery. I knew when I was a bit pathetic at things and delegating would work in both our favors.

Since I still had some time before dinner, though, I decided to also check out Walter's room. It was probably already cleaned, and that made me think of the fact that Norm potentially did not know about this new wrinkle in Penny's family fabric unless someone had told him. I hadn't seen him take any statements just yet, and as far as I knew, he was still hiding the murder aspect of Penny's death from the family. I wasn't sure what to make of that at this point, but I wasn't going to change his story for him.

Heading up to the third floor, I didn't take the back stairs again. It didn't make sense, since I would have had to exit the painting and risk getting caught just to mount the next set of stairs around the corner. Not to mention, I didn't know if Glennis was still crying in the kitchen. Without any new information on my side, I wouldn't be able to make her feel better. And if she wasn't willing to share anything new with me, we might end up at odds again, and I didn't want that.

I checked my phone to see if Mena had managed to get the recipe pictures yet, but there was nothing new from her either. Had her thrall worn off on Micah as soon as he'd left her magnetic space? I sure as heck hoped not. Because I had a feeling that if I could get the images to Glennis that she might be triggered into telling me something, anything, that could possibly help with the debacle we found ourselves in.

I took my time going up the stairs. The second set was just as arduous and even more narrow. Telling myself I was trying to save my strength worked for a few steps. I didn't normally go up and down the stairs for anything, but apparently today was just a different kind of day. It made me think for just a second about installing an elevator, but the expense was astronomical, and I had no idea where I'd actually put one. Not to mention, there was every possibility that it would damage the interior of the house. I did have downstairs rooms that I reserved for anyone who could not navigate the stairs, so I didn't really need one, necessarily.

And what if they wanted to put it in, and it destroyed the secret closet under the stairs where a pay phone from forever ago resided? It no longer worked for outside calls from what I'd been told, but it was where I could get a hold of Earl, the resident ghost.

I mentally put talking to him on my list for after everyone had gone to bed. I needed to know if he'd had a conversation with Amelia, and I needed to tell him not to interact with her again. She wasn't ready yet, and I didn't want to force her into anything without first talking to her dad about her capabilities.

So many things were going on, and what felt like so little time to actually handle any of it.

But I had leads to follow, rooms to visit, and apparently teddies to find.

I didn't meet anyone on my way up to the third floor, and I gusted out a sigh of relief when I arrived on the landing. I peeked back down the stairs, just to make sure no one had followed me up, and then I let myself into Walter's room. Once I was in, I closed and locked the door behind me.

I was on the hunt for anything and everything he might have left behind. Usually, most people were pretty good about grabbing all their belongings before leaving. I had even seen people bring out a very detailed list of every single thing they had packed, including a line that stated suitcase. Not sure how you would leave without your suitcase if you had all the other items on your list, but it could happen, I suppose. And this was one of those times that I really hoped he had forgotten something.

Maybe he had killed Penny and had run so fast that he'd forgotten a teddy bear? Was it one she'd given him?

For the first time ever, I felt weird going into one of the rooms in my very own establishment. I wasn't sure what I felt when I opened the door, but it definitely had an edge of being uncomfortable. Of being watched, though I couldn't have told you why.

The bed was a queen, covered in a bedspread Poobah had commissioned in the nineties with the hex symbols that were often found in Pennsylvania Dutch country. It was a lovely shade of cream, embroidered with symbols that graced barns and homes in Lancaster County and other parts of the state. It was straight and covered the mattress beautifully. Since the housekeeping staff hadn't been in yet, Walter must have made the bed himself with a whopping dollop of precision from the way the corners were knife-pleated at the end. It would still have to be taken apart, washed, and then remade, but I did appreciate his attention to detail.

Poking around throughout the room didn't get me much. As I searched, I found that he had been careful to put everything back to rights, though maybe it was a little too back to rights. Every surface had been wiped down, and there was a slight tinge of antiseptic wipes lingering in the air near the dresser. Had he taken precautions and wiped down every piece of furniture? Was he making an effort to get rid of his fingerprints? Why? Even the trash can next to the desk was empty.

I wandered around some more and then finally had to admit that there was literally nothing here. Maybe he was just that clean of a person. He wouldn't be the first, and I highly doubted he'd be the last. We had quite a few guests who asked for disinfectant wipes to be brought to the room, even though they said the room was very nice and clean. They just needed to do it themselves because it made them feel better. We'd even had one guest bring all her own linens, including sheets, blankets, and towels. To each person their own. I wouldn't stop you if it made you feel more at home. But between the cleaning and the feeling of being watched, I was all too happy to finally leave, even though I was leaving empty-handed. Again.

Back to square one, or one and a half, since I did have several other people to look into, and a memoir to see if I could find any trace of. As a librarian, Penny had to have posted something somewhere about what she was doing. Maybe that would create some threads, no matter how fragile, that I could follow.

I'd admit, though, that I was feeling a little defeated. What room? This one? Penny's? The dining room? What teddy? At this point, I'd almost take the lingerie if it had some note on it that told me where to look next.

I could go back to the library and see if there was another book sparkling. At this point, I was willing to go another round just to start putting some clues together. I was halfway down the first set of stairs when my phone pinged with a message from Mena. I had a special ringtone just for her, and it made me giggle when it sang out. Nothing like tromping down the stairs to a clip of Westley saying, "As you wish."

And when I opened my phone, there was the information I'd been hoping for. Two pictures, one of the front of the recipe card and one of the back. I hit the first with my finger, and then blew it up to look over every inch of it, trying to see what would have been so important that it required secrecy and her own nephew thinking she might have murdered to get it back. I found nothing. Three for three did not seem to be working in my favor. Maybe four for four?

I pressed on the second picture and blew that one up, too, using my fingertip to move from left to right, back and forth over the script on the card. At first, I didn't see anything that made sense. It was a series of words that didn't seem to go together. They weren't formed into sentences. They weren't stacked in a way that would make me think they were a riddle, either. What the heck was I looking at?

My desire to run down the rest of the stairs, grab Glennis, then make her explain to me what this was, nearly overwhelmed me. But then I remembered who I'd be dealing with and how she felt about this card from the get-go, and I forced myself to stop skipping down the stairs after the fourth one. It landed me on the stair that held the lever for opening the door to the secret phone booth below.

I wanted to talk to Earl to see if he'd noticed anything around the inn, and also if he had been in contact with the deceased at all. He'd done it before, but I wasn't sure if he could do it every time. It was, however, worth my time and attention to ask. Besides, I still needed to speak with him about Amelia. Midnight was the best time for that, so I had hours to go until sleep.

Aunt Hellen was at the desk when I finally reached the lobby this time, and she was dealing with one of Penny's kids. I gestured to see if she needed help, and she gave a sharp shake of her head. Okay, then. On to Glennis. To say I was both excited to ask and dreading asking was a true statement, but I was going to have to find that middle ground and do what needed to be done.

Except I miscalculated the time, and when I walked into the kitchen, it was absolutely bustling with my three ladies working at the stoves, the prep counters, and digging into the refrigerator. I nearly got mowed down as Clara turned from the prep counter with a bounty of salad items all cradled in a basket she'd made with her apron.

"You can't be in here right now, Roxy. I'm not trying to be difficult, but we had some requests from the front desk for dinner. And I'll be damned if I don't fulfill them after how they shut me out for meals during their stay." Glennis waved a hand at me to shoo me out, and I decided perhaps the card could wait until tomorrow. I had other avenues to look at, and I really did not want it to be Glennis.

So maybe I should use the hours before midnight to do research on the people who were actually staying in the building. My thought was that they would have far more motivation to kill a relative than my cook, who'd never met the family before, as far as she'd said.

I backed out slowly, staying out of Taylor's way as she emerged from the refrigerator, also with her hands full.

"You must have had quite the time at the grocery store," I said, my mind quickly tallying up what she had probably spent there. Normally, we'd get shipments from suppliers, since that was less expensive than buying right off the shelf. But there had been no company that could supply us that quickly, and no need to buy in bulk when everyone was going to be out of here as soon as this thing was solved.

So much for my budget for this month, although Penny had paid full rate and hadn't taken advantage of the food included in the price. So, I was technically still in the black when it came to finances.

Mena was standing in the hallway when I backed out of the kitchen, and she grabbed my arm before I could even say hi.

"We need to talk. There's something more going on here that I don't understand. Have you gotten any messages that don't make sense? My Spidey senses are tingling, but for the first time in a very long time, I can't put my finger on why."

"Maybe we should take this to my rooms." I shot a look over to the front desk, where Hellen had moved from one set of guests to the next. What exactly were they looking for? I could have asked, but I didn't want to get involved when I had other things to do. Aunt Hellen would let me know if she needed me. Other than that, she was incredibly capable, and the guests would get better service from her than me, probably, right now.

I let Mena drag me to my rooms. And by drag, I did literally mean drag. I was walking as fast as I could, but Mena wanted me to run, and she wasn't getting that. I tried to pull her back the first few steps, so that we could walk sedately, and she was having none of that.

But even when I picked up the pace, it wasn't enough for her, and she just kept getting faster and faster.

"This is not a freaking sprint, Mena. Slow your freaking roll!"

"This is a sprint, Roxy, and we need to get into your rooms now so I can tell you all the things I found out. We've got a lot of work to do, and we'll be faster at doing it if you'll stop with your turtle crawl and get hopping along the hallway. Come on!"

Her urgency resonated in me. I didn't know if it was her trying to use her talent on me, or if it really was just a need for speed, but I picked up the pace as best as I could in my heels. I was not going to face plant in the hallway in front of everyone just so that she could tell me that Micah fancied her, and wasn't that fun? Especially when it got her what she wanted?

As soon as I entered the room, Mena slammed the door behind me, then leaned back against it like she had run a marathon from danger and had finally found a safe place. Her dramatics could be a little much, in case you hadn't noticed.

"Penny was a cougar, which I have no issue with, but she was also taping everything that happened in her room, and Micah thinks they may have footage of someone coming in and going through all her things. They caught it on a nanny cam hidden in a teddy bear in her room!"

Oh, now, that could be something.

Chapter 10

"A teddy bear in her room?" That could totally fit the message the book had given me, and I was here for that. It gave me hope that I could stop feeling like I just hadn't gotten the message. Answers were my best friends sometimes. Now, if only I could figure out what to do with this information, or maybe at least know what was on the footage. That would help immensely.

"Yes! It's all on there!" She clapped her hands.

"But the murder happened in the library with the candlestick."

"Don't ruin my glee over this new clue, Roxy Gleason. I'm riding high on something working finally."

I gave her a smile. "You say that like we've been working on this for years. It literally hasn't even been twelve hours."

She pushed away from the door and took a seat on my couch in the sitting room. "Fair enough, but this is also putting off my vacation, so every minute feels like an hour until I leave."

"You want to be away from here so bad?" I took a seat farther down the couch from her and cradled a throw pillow against my stomach.

She groaned. "No, you weirdo. I want to see some sights and spend some time with our parents. Give you a chance to actually believe that life with Dean would be a vast improvement over life without him. And then I'll come back and fall right into being that irritating little sister you love, as I keep asking when he's going to propose, then." She crossed her legs and spread her arms out over the back of the couch, like she owned the thing.

"I haven't thought that far ahead yet." I had, actually, but I wasn't going to admit to it.

"That's what you have me for." She dropped her arms and then folded her hands in her lap. "Micah found quite a bit of information, surprisingly. I did my best and scored, just FYI, to convince him that if he wanted Norm to be a happy camper, it would behoove him to share that very information with us, or at least me. That way, I could get to the bottom of things and hand the whole killer to him in a wrapped bow, so I could get out of here. Of course, I also told him that the sooner I leave, the sooner I can come back, and that made things get a little heated." Her smile was pure mischief.

Oh, my word. "What do you mean by 'heated'? As in you were yelling at each other?"

"Oh, my dear Roxy." She patted my leg and sat back, as if she were in her throne. "There's more than one way to bring the heat. We'll leave that for the moment, though, because there are things I need to tell you, and I don't want to get off track." She grabbed the pen and paper from the coffee table in front of her and started writing. Or was she drawing?

I couldn't tell. But I did know, if I pushed her, that she'd just ram her heels into the ground and not let me see anything until she was good and ready to share it. She could be incredibly difficult, but she was also incredibly smart, and so I waited.

Eventually, what felt like eighty-two minutes later, but was probably eighty-two seconds, she turned the notepad to me. "Micah wouldn't let me take the photo of the person with me, but I was able to do my best to remember every angle and wrinkle."

What she showed me wasn't exactly a portrait. In fact, it looked more like a Picasso than a Rembrandt. But maybe if I looked at it long enough, it would make sense. There was something a little affirming, though, to see that she couldn't do everything well...

I cleared my throat because I was literally speechless.

She sighed. "Yeah, it sucks, okay? I know it sucks, and everyone else will think it sucks. The picture is right in my head, but that obviously did not translate well through the pencil."

I nudged her with my shoulder. "I mean, you have to have at least one flaw, right? Or the world would collapse under the amazingness of your awesomeness."

She thought for a minute, trying to turn the picture left and right. "There is some truth to that. I wouldn't want to unbalance the world. But even though I can't draw the guy, I would totally know him if I saw him. I just have to be on the lookout."

"Well, let me know if you see anyone who matches that..." I tipped my head toward her drawing, and this time she giggled.

"Yeah, I don't think I'll be showing it to anyone." She took one last look at it and then crumpled it up.

I grabbed it from her and smoothed it back out. "No, don't do that! There is every possibility that there is actually something in here that will click into place at some point, so we don't want to throw away any ideas and clues."

She blew out a breath, but then she smiled. "I appreciate you trying to make me feel better, but I doubt it. However, you keep it if you think it might help."

"Will do. Now, we need to think about how to present these pictures of the recipe card to Glennis, but also get some info out of her. I don't want to just tell her we have them without something first."

"That's manipulation!" She cackled. "I like it."

"Of course you do." I brought the pictures back up on my phone. "So how should we approach her? I feel like I have to be the one to do this, even though you would be far more qualified. This is something I promised I would do for her, and it is going to weigh hard in my favor for us to get some more of her story out."

"Can't disagree with that."

Finally, I felt like we might be on a good path and in a place to get some answers. I hoped I was right, because I really needed a win here. Please and thank you.

"So, should I corner her once dinner is served, and tell her I have something of value she wants, and then get her to promise to help me before I show her?"

"Amateur," Mena said, then proceeded to school me on how it was really done.

***

Have you ever been so ready for something, and yet, completely behind the eight ball, with no real idea how you were going to accomplish said thing? Yeah, that was me right now. Knowing what I had to do, I was sure that I knew how to do it, but not entirely certain that I could actually pull it off.

But I was still going to try, because this was important, and that meant I just had to get out of my own way. Right. Battle-ready and willing, that was me.

I checked in on the family in the dining room through the open door as I passed. Everyone seemed to be pretty sedate.

Though that made sense. They had just experienced a death in the family this morning, even if they didn't know yet how it had occurred, and no one knew who had done it, except the murderer.

Since no one was throwing food and voices were not raised, I did not actually poke my head in to see how things were going. From their constant stream to the front desk, I was confident they would let us know if something was wrong.

Stepping past the door, I straightened my shirt, smoothed down my skirt, and pushed a hand through my short hair. I could do this. Heck, I'd done it before, kind of, and now I had been schooled by a pro. I would do this.

Taking a breath, I listened at the door for a second before pushing it open. It was important that everyone was in there, not just me and Glennis. I had a better chance of forcing her hand at the outset if we had an audience, per Mena.

And an audience we did have, as I stepped in to find not only my three kitchen ladies, but also Uncle Vince, Poobah, and Aunt Hellen.

"What are we all doing in here?" I asked, looking around the room and into each face.

"Shhh," Aunt Hellen said. "We're waiting through what feels like a commercial break for the snarking to begin again."

"The what? Everyone is calm out there. They're quiet because they lost a matriarch today. I just looked in, and everyone is quiet. You can see it on the TV right there, too."

"You walked by at the one second in the last thirty minutes that they haven't been lobbing insults at each other and gesticulating wildly," Aunt Hellen said. "We've been taking shifts listening at the door and reporting back. We have bets going at this point to see who will say what next. I wanted bingo cards, but my idea was shut down as taking too long to put together.

But if they're going to be here through more meals, then I'm going to do it myself."

The silence in the dining room was deafening now, even though the TV had no sound. "I'm sure you'll come up with something," I said absently, as I looked at the screen, trying to see what was going on, but coming up empty. "What is it that they've been fighting about?"

"Someone told them Penny was murdered an hour ago, and they all have different ideas on who did it and why." Poobah leaned back against the counter to my left, never taking his eyes off the television.

"Most of them want to stay until the murderer is caught, even though it could happen to them here," Clara said, also not taking her eyes off the screen. "But, according to Sally, at least here they are more on high alert and not settling back into daily life. But they're trying to figure out who is going to pay for what, because some have jobs and need to get home, and some only are here because someone else paid for them to have a vacation."

"Don't you dare think about offering them a discount, Roxy," Aunt Hellen said before I even thought about it.

I bristled a little, but then settled right down. She was right, and I had already given them a free night tonight. They could absolutely pay for anything more, especially since I had to pay my staff to stick around for longer if this didn't get solved quickly, and we weren't done in time for them all to leave on their vacations.

What a pain in the keister!

"I won't. However, I think I should probably go in there and see what they're doing and saying. That way, I can start offering solutions, instead of waiting for them to come to conclusions on their own. I'd rather they be here, because that way I can keep an eye on them. It has to be one of them who killed Penny. Who else would have done it, and why?" I made a point not to look at

Glennis, but I did see Clara shift her eyes for just a second. When she brought them back to find me looking at her, her shoulders rose toward her ears.

I needed to figure this out soon for a number of reasons, but mainly to prove that it wasn't Glennis, because if I couldn't prove that, I had a feeling we'd be in for some rocky times in the kitchen.

"I'll be back." I straightened my already straight blouse and skirt and girded my loins as best I could, though I wasn't very good at that. Except that wasn't entirely true. I'd dealt with difficult people before. I could deal with them now. It was just that there were so many other moving parts of this whole thing that I felt some of the balls slipping out of my hands. I was afraid one of them might shatter on the floor before I could save it.

There was a general murmur of approval as I slapped a hand onto the kitchen door leading out to the hallway and marched through. Decisive and concise was needed here, no pandering. I could be firm without being mean, and that was the flavor I was going for as I stepped into the dining room, and everyone went quiet.

"Good evening, I hope you're all enjoying the meal Glennis provided." I did the more melancholy smile instead of the bright beam of light one, since it was still somber in the room, no matter what they had been fighting about.

"It's wonderful," Jessica said. "I'm only sorry that Penny did not allow us to have Glennis provide all our meals while we were here. Everything else was fine, and we were never hungry. But if this is what your cook can do with tortellini, then I'll look forward to what she can do with other foods, as we're extending our stay, and we'd like to have all meals included." She nodded her head, as if that was the last word on that.

I caught Leon frowning out of the corner of my eye, but I didn't look at him. Jessica didn't either, but she had to know that he was not a happy camper. She didn't seem to care, though, and yet Sally looked incredibly pleased, despite the reasons they were staying.

That was a lot easier than I had thought it would be.

"Of course," I said. "We're here to accommodate whatever you need. How long do you plan to extend your stay?" And who was paying for it? I wanted to ask that second question, but there was time enough for that later. Although the only credit card we had on file would be in Penny's name, and we couldn't charge that now that she was gone.

"I would like to do a day-by-day. I believe that should work for you." Jessica did not sound like she was going to brook any arguments on that. Since that was what I would have preferred, anyway, I simply closed my eyes and then nodded as if she had won. The smile on her face made me cringe, but only internally. This was one of those times that I would let her think she won. It cost me nothing. In fact, it would make me more money than I had thought it would if I were to have offered a solution. So that was good.

"Are you all paying for the rooms individually? I can have Hellen come out and put credit cards on file for each."

This time, Leon couldn't keep his groan in, and his frown turned into a fierce scowl. Sally laid a hand on his forearm. After shaking her off, he threw his linen napkin on the table, shoved his chair back, and stalked out of the room.

"I'll put everyone's room on my credit card. Thank you for asking." Jessica didn't look thankful that I'd pushed the issue in front of everyone, but that was business.

I left before anything else could be said and went directly back to the kitchen without hesitation. I'd catch Jessica once everyone else had left the table. Right now, I wanted to go up the back stairs to see if I could hear Leon swearing, and if he let loose anything that might help my investigation.

"If you see Jessica leave, make sure you grab her before she goes upstairs. She's putting the rooms on her card, and they're going to go one day at a time, thankfully. Which means we have to step up the information gathering." Again, I avoided looking at Glennis, but this time several pairs of eyes shifted her way before glancing back toward me. I knew what they were thinking, because I was thinking it, too. How was I going to get Glennis to talk? She had to know something. But I had that card up my sleeve. Well, actually, it was in my pocket on my phone, but that was just semantics. And I was going to use that card, just as soon as I got everyone else to leave. I was changing my plan from wanting witnesses to wanting her alone. Mena might know how to manipulate with the best of them, but I needed to do this my way and geared toward the woman I'd known for my whole life.

"Clara and Taylor, why don't you go start cleaning up? It looks like people might be drifting off soon since they've all eaten, and the lodging question is answered. Aunt Hellen, if you could man the front desk or linger outside the dining room, that would be awesome. Poobah and Uncle Vance, if you could make sure that Aunt Hellen isn't railroaded, that would be very helpful."

I didn't really need the two men to handle Hellen, and we all knew it, but no one fought. Poobah did raise an eyebrow at me, but he could just keep wondering for all I cared right now.

"Mena, stay at the door here if you could. I'm going to go up to see if I can hear anything."

Everyone scurried to do what I asked them to do. It was probably better defined as sauntering, but I preferred to think of it as scurrying, because it made me feel like I was actually being listened to just this once. That was also not fair. So, to actually be fair, they often listened to me. But I was feeling a little feisty.

Opening the door at the bottom of the back stairs, I entered and then shut the door behind me. I crept up the stairs, listening for anything that might be happening above near Leon and Sally's room.

At first, I didn't hear anything at all. The whole upstairs appeared to be quiet, but then I heard some banging around and gently opened the painting at the top of the stairs, just a little bit, in order to get a better listening post.

"Stupid, stupid, stupid! Why do I even have to be here? And why is this dragging on? So, she died. We don't have to stay here when she's dead. She was old and finally!" He yelled that last word, and I wondered at the significance.

She really wasn't that old, from what I could tell. No more than her sixties, and yet he thought she should have been dead already? That seemed odd. Or had he set things up before to take her out, and none of them had worked, but this one had?

"If that bitch thinks that I'm going to let her ruin my career and my life again, then she has some serious issues, because that is not the way this is going to go down."

Who was he talking about? His wife? Jessica? Penny's memory? There was no way to tell, and I was not in a position to ask him for clarification. I eased the door closed when he started muttering to himself again, fumbling with the key in the door.

"Stupid hotel! Stupid vacation! Idiotic women!" I could hear him escalating his volume and anger through the painting, and it was not pretty.

"That's enough," a woman said from the other side of the door, and I so wished I hadn't closed it. I didn't think it sounded like Sally, and now I couldn't exactly open the door and peek out without getting caught. Dang it!

Chapter 11

No matter how much I wanted to clatter down the stairs and look up from the bottom of the front staircase to see who he was talking to. But more than that, I didn't want to get caught, so I stayed put. I'd have to ask Hellen who she saw go up the stairs after Leon, and hope it was only one person, and not a bunch.

A door slammed, and I could no longer hear anyone talking. I took that as my sign that my mission here was accomplished, even if it left me with more questions than answers. Hopefully, questions that would get me answers that could move this whole thing forward.

Toward the bottom of the stairs, I lost my hesitation and flew down the rest, whipping the door open into the kitchen. Except, I did not think until the very last second that I had asked Mena to stand guard, which meant I hit her with my stunt.

"Oops, sorry!"

"Ow, you know you could be a little more careful."

"You're absolutely right, and I'll apologize in just a second. I have to know who followed Leon upstairs." I scooted her out of the way and made a beeline for Aunt Hellen. Unfortunately, she was talking with Jessica, so I couldn't exactly interrupt them.

Instead, I, very casually, walked up the stairs and found Sally at the top, trying to get into her room.

"Freaking door! What is it with this place?" She yanked on the handle and turned the key again, but she couldn't seem to get the door to budge.

"Is there a problem?" I asked, as if I hadn't been standing there long enough to know what she was trying to do.

"Ha! There's more than one problem, and you know it. The biggest one, at the moment, though, is that your stupid key isn't working. This happened to me a couple of days ago, too. Why does it work sometimes and not others? Don't you have maintenance?"

"I do, and I find it odd that the key doesn't work only sometimes. Did you let Hellen know when it happened before?"

"No." She shot me a narrow-eyed look. "It opened, eventually, so I thought maybe I just wasn't turning it all the way. But then Leon opened the door from inside, and the key worked every other time after that."

That could be the problem—that Leon was somehow blocking the door, and it had nothing to do with the key. But I wasn't going to be the one to say that. "Maybe try it again? Or I can knock and see if he can open it from the inside again?"

"Is he in there? How do you know if he's in there?"

I did not want to answer that, so I just stepped in front of her and knocked, calling out to see if he could open the door. "Leon, we appear to be stuck out here, and something is wrong with the doorknob. Could you please open it from your side?"

Something hit the ground with a thump, and then he whipped the door open a second later. I tried to peer into the room to see if the woman I'd heard talking to him earlier was still in there with him. She was nowhere to be seen, but I didn't know how she would have gotten out. I'd had someone try to walk the very narrow ledge outside the window last year. He'd fallen through the roof below. Hopefully, they hadn't tried that. But where was she?

A shadow moved at the edge of the bed, and the heel of a pink pump disappeared under the bed skirt. Who was that? Who had had those shoes on earlier? I couldn't remember, but I could probably find out if I asked Mena. She paid attention to those kinds of things.

Now, I had two trains of thought on this. I could call out the person hiding under the bed and force them to show themselves, or I could wait to see what happened if I took Sally downstairs with me.

"Actually, Sally, I'm sure you were hoping to probably turn in soon. I know it's been a long and emotionally rough day. But would you mind coming back to the dining room and meeting with Hellen? I thought you might be the best person to run tomorrow's menu by. I know there are some particular tastes in your group, and you always seem to be the one who knows things." Nothing wrong with a little flattery to get her moving in the direction I was aiming for.

"Does it have to be now?" The slight tinge of whining didn't go unnoticed. But I needed her to leave, and this was the only way I knew how to get her to do it.

"It does. Glennis works better when she knows what to expect. She'll have to go to the grocery store, since we didn't place a big order with all of your meals being taken elsewhere. If we could at least make up tomorrow's menu, and then give me some options for other things that we could be ready for, that would be wonderful. If you don't mind, of course."

I could tell that she did mind, as she took her hand off the doorknob and swiveled back to me, waving her hand for me to go first. She didn't even say goodbye to Leon, and he was quick to close the door as soon as she turned her back.

I let Sally get about halfway down the stairs before I texted Aunt Hellen to let her know Sally was incoming, and I needed her to keep her busy for at least ten minutes. She texted back a thumbs-up sign. A second later, she greeted Sally at the bottom of the stairs, whisking her off to the dining room. Breathing a quiet sigh of relief, I quickly opened the painting at the top of the stairs and left the door ajar so I could see who came out of Leon's room wearing those pink heels.

I stood there for all of about fifteen seconds when Leon cracked the door open, poked his head out, and then opened the door wider when he thought the coast was clear. And then he shoved Jessica's daughter-in-law, Sylvie, out the door and closed it behind her, while she stumbled in those heels, then righted herself. She smoothed down her pencil skirt and turned back to the door with a frown, grumbling under her breath. I so wished I could hear what she was saying, but her identity would have to be enough. At least it was more than I had before.

Now I had to get downstairs and see what their ties were, and why Leon would feel the need to hide her from his own wife.

Something was fishy in the Charmed Inn, and it was about time for me to dive into why and sort out the pieces I had, then start asking questions of a number of people.

I was careful when I opened the kitchen door this time, not wanting to slam anyone else into the wall, as I'd done earlier. Only Glennis was in the room when I closed the door behind me. I'd been hoping, but hadn't put too much stock into the possibility. She could have chosen to leave with everyone else, and yet she was there, tucking her apron into the laundry basket while keeping an eye on the menu planning going on in the dining room between Sally and Aunt Hellen.

I didn't want to scare her, so I called out in a softer voice than normal while I quietly closed the door behind me. She still jumped, but no one could say I hadn't made an effort.

"Roxy, you need to be better at announcing yourself." She slapped a hand to her chest and blew out a breath. "I'm heading out. Or did you want me to stay until Hellen is done talking with that woman out there?"

That woman out there. Why did that sound somewhat ominous?

"I was trying to make things easier for you because they're staying through tonight and tomorrow night and are asking to have all the meals made. Jessica even said that she wished they'd had all their meals made here because breakfast and dinner were so good." Again, with the stroking of ego to get what I needed. Was this the manipulation I always accused Mena of doing? I guess as long as it worked, there was nothing wrong with it, and at least this time I was being completely sincere.

"So, do you think it was Penny that didn't want me to cook for them? Why? Did she see some review of bad food or something?" Glennis looked vulnerable for the first time in a long time, not mad or cocky, but truly vulnerable.

"I don't actually know. I didn't take their reservation when Penny made the request, but I can ask Hellen if any reason was given for not wanting the food service. I thought it was just because they wanted to explore the town and what it had to offer."

"I don't know, but she gave me some strange looks the few times I did see her. There was an edge to her smile that made me uncomfortable, but I didn't know if I was just imagining it, so I didn't say anything. Now, I'm not so sure if she didn't have some grudge against me. I've been trying to think of if I'd ever met her before, but I can't recall, unless she's a previous guest here? We have so many that it's possible, yet you'd think I'd remember."

It was the perfect lead in to ask her what she'd been crying about earlier, and if there was any way she'd finally tell me what she knew, but I didn't take it. Instead, I removed my phone from my pocket and hoped with everything I had that she might give me some information once I showed her the recipe card.

"Mena was able to talk with the station and get some pictures that might jog your brain." I swiped up on my phone to access my text app.

"I don't want to see anything dead." The panic in her voice shot through me, and I looked up to find tears standing in her eyes.

"No, I wasn't going to show you dead bodies." I sighed. I couldn't do this. "Mena got the pictures of the front and back of the recipe card. I'll forward them to you, and if you think of any reason why Penny would have had that card with her when she was killed, then it would be really helpful if you'd share any ideas with me."

She grabbed her phone out of her purse and waited impatiently while I downloaded the pictures and then texted them to her as attachments.

She kept refreshing her screen as soon as I hit send. "Come on!" she said under her breath.

"What is it about the card that is so important? I get that it's an old recipe that's been in your family for years, but why is that so significant?"

Except the pictures had finally landed on her phone, so she brushed me off and hustled out the back door from the kitchen. I watched as she took up a seat in the gazebo and kept swiping her pointer finger left and right over the screen of her phone.

I did the same thing. I still couldn't figure out what the draw was or what, if anything, I was looking at. The front had a flower border like recipes from long ago. My grandmother used to have recipe parties around the holidays, and everyone would bring ten of the same recipes to share with the other ladies attending the party. Each would also bring the made food item. The cookies and casseroles were often plentiful and delicious. I remembered this particular kind of card, but that didn't mean anything. And the recipe was for some French dish that I wasn't even going to try to pronounce. It looked pretty straightforward, with the ingredients listed first and then the individual steps to put it together. The baking time and oven temperature weren't exactly iconic either, so what was the big deal? Maybe that was on the back.

I swiped and looked again at the back of the card. Nothing struck me when I looked over the words again. It was just a bunch of words that didn't make any real sense, no sentences, no rhythm to what was written. They weren't stacked like a poem and had no real cohesiveness. What was she looking at, and how did this make sense to her?

The desire to ask her was incredibly strong. However, her shoulders started shaking, and I just couldn't do it to her right now. I had a lot of other information to work through. I would do that first before I drill down on her. The need to know what these words on the back meant to her was stark. But it could be a false lead, and I would feel horrible for having pinned her down, only to find out that Penny's death had nothing to do with the card.

Looking out beyond the gazebo, I could see Caper and Dean playing keep away with Caper's kids. I had no idea what they were throwing back and forth between the two adults, and I couldn't hear the laughter, but there was no denying they were having a lot of fun.

So, interesting how the world ran in so many different emotional circles all at once.

I turned from the window. Leaving Glennis to her own thoughts and feelings and Dean and his family with their joy, I took myself back to my room and got ready to dig into as much information as I could. I wasn't necessarily good at internet research. In fact, I might be doing some of what Isaac would do so much better. But I had to do something until midnight, when I could talk with Earl and see what he had seen or heard as he hung around the inn.

Mena's text ringtone sounded as the kitchen door swung shut behind me. She was asking if I'd talked to Glennis. I answered that I had, and that I didn't have anything new, but I would tomorrow. She sent back a frowny face, and I hit her with a thumbs up and told her to leave it to me.

She might not, and I braced myself for that, but I could only worry about so many things at once.

I didn't meet anyone on my way back to my rooms, and I didn't hear anyone. Maybe the grief of the day had sent everyone off to their rooms to just kind of hide in their caves for the night. It was late and dark outside, too. I had expected them to maybe be in the game room or something, but as I passed it and looked in, the pool table was untouched. It reminded me of the conversation I'd had with Poobah and my feelings about the book I wanted to see and what he expected me to do before he'd show it to me. Plus, I still didn't know what Glennis had over him.

When I got to my door, I opened it quickly, then closed it just as quickly behind me. No one was following me, so there was no reason to have done that, but I felt like I was gaining momentum as I walked through the doorway. I was going to go with it.

I flipped the switch to start the electric tea kettle and set out my favorite mug and tea bag. Spooning out some sugar, I measured out my normal amount and then dropped in a little bit more, just because I could. The whole time, so many things were running through my head. I needed to make a list of all the players, even the kids. I needed to think about the different questions I wanted answered. Where did they all live? I felt like it was not close to each other. Since they had all stayed here. And I doubted they would have all done that, even on Penny's dime, if they lived close. Did they all live in the same area, or were they all over the country? I figured no one had flown in, or they would not have been okay with staying longer, since they might not have been able to change their flights.

Okay, that was good info and a good track to start with. Then I needed to look into what kind of work each of them was involved in. Where the kids might go to school. Some of the questions were not going to be answered on the internet, since they might have done as much as they could to keep the kids' personal information off the sites. And I highly doubted the toddler had anything to do with things, but I'd still put him on the list because he would have connections that might make something pop as I put things together.

The teakettle switch clicked, and I was thankful that it wasn't a whistle. I probably would have jumped like Glennis had earlier in the kitchen. She was another one that I was going to see if I could glean anything new about her. I could at least ask around to a few people in town to see what they knew about her from her youth. Maybe they'd tell me if they had noticed anything recently that I might need to know about, but didn't because I'd had my head in the clouds about Dean.

Although, to be fair to myself, I didn't tend to look into my employees' lives outside of the inn for things they didn't want to tell me, normally. But this was not a normal time, and that was a now thing, not a last week thing.

I made a list of people whom I thought might have some information and what questions I'd ask. Definitely Mrs. Lincoln, who lived on the riverfront, and maybe Nancy Braden down at the bakery where Uncle Vince always got the donuts. She'd been around for a long time, and she and Glennis were of the same age. She could be a good source of gossip, and she loved her gossip, so it wouldn't be that far out of the realm of possibility that I'd be asking. I usually stayed around the inn and let other people go out and do the things I needed, like getting food or checking in with the suppliers in the area, because we liked to keep it as local as possible.

I was going to have to step out of my comfort zone if I wanted this solved in any reasonable time, though. Because, as much as I appreciated the extra money from having guests that I hadn't expected, I also had vacations on the calendar and did not want to mess those up for my staff.

After I doctored my tea the way I liked it, with plenty of cream from my small dorm room-sized refrigerator, I sat down with my computer.

Just as I suspected, I could look people up on a search engine like anyone else, but I only got surface information. Penny had charity events that she had total control over as the top organizer, and a series of awards for being an outstanding citizen. Someone could have been jealous of everything she seemed to be honored for, even though you could tell there was no way she was doing it all by herself. Yet she thanked no one else in her acceptance speeches. But her town was almost ninety minutes away. I highly doubted that anyone had driven that far just to murder her on her vacation. I wasn't ruling it out, so I did put it on the possible, but not probable page. Due diligence, you understand.

Penny's daughters, Rebecca and Francis, who had come alone, both appeared to have pretty standard social lives. Rebecca was a photographer, and she had a real eye for wildlife, but never posted pictures of herself. She held a job at an accounting firm, and there was very little else I found on her. Francis, on the other hand, seemed to be the flying-high one, with numerous posts about her nights out on the town with what seemed like a revolving group of friends. She went to concerts and plays and movies, constantly telling people, at length, what she thought of every single one, from production value to makeup and cos-tuming, briefly touching on the acting or performance. So, lots of surface, but not a lot of substance. That didn't mean there wasn't far more to her than what she posted online, but I made some notes and moved on to Jerrod, Penny's son.

I couldn't find him online, which seemed weird, but wasn't necessarily weird enough to call it out. Though I would have expected at least something, since he was an up-and-coming graphic designer, from what some of Penny's posts had talked about when she had him do a spread for her with her accomplishments. I would have thought he'd have far more online due to the very nature of his business, but it was possible he was just getting started. I knew next to nothing about graphic design, other than that our logo was made about a hundred years ago, and I wasn't allowed to change it. I didn't want to, but I was told that from the very beginning by Poobah.

Poobah, who was still sitting at the back of my mind. Why wouldn't he tell me what he knew about Glennis so I could clear her and get into who could have been the real culprit?

I deliberately set that aside because I did not have the time for it right now, and I had no way of asking, since he would have gone to bed hours ago in his own home down the road.

Glancing up at the clock, I saw I had about fifteen minutes before I planned to call Earl and see what I could get him to tell me.

I quickly breezed through several articles about Sally and her husband Leon. He was some kind of international law pro-fessor. Had he been concerned then about getting his classes sorted out before the next quarter? What other businessman stuff was Sally asking him to forgo for this vacation? What was so important that he felt the need to leave right away, even before the actual checkout time?

Sally was all about her kids, and I loved seeing so many smiling pictures. But I knew there was something behind the scenes there when not a single picture or memory involved Leon. Why not?

I had no way of knowing without asking her, or leaving it to Isaac and his deft amateur private investigator skills, so I made a list of questions and moved on.

Penny's sister Jessica had no real social media presence, but she had been a chief nurse at a very large hospital and was praised often for her commitment to healing patients. She'd even written a book to guide nurses through their training with childhood cancer and was touted as one of the best in the world. Was that why Penny had wanted to write a book, and Jessica couldn't let other people share her spotlight?

So many questions! And I still had to look at Jessica's family, including Sylvie, whom I had seen sneaking out of Leon's room after hiding under the bed so as not to be caught by Sally. What was going on there?

Sylvie's husband was John, and they had two older teens, Tom and Trevor. And finally, there was Michael, Jessica's last son, whom she had turned to earlier to discuss the funeral arrangements before I'd cut them all off by asking about that memoir Penny had been writing. The one Jessica said had no place being written, much less published, because it had to do with something that should never have happened.

I had about five minutes left, so I tried looking for any info on Penny related to the memoir. I bookmarked a couple of pages to come back to because they did mention her name and her teaching a class about writing memoirs. They didn't mention her own memoir, but maybe I would know more about what to ask the search engine once I'd talked to Earl.

It was certainly worth a try since nothing else seemed to be panning out.

Chapter 12

I was careful to be as quiet as possible when I triggered the latch on the staircase to open the door for the phone booth. It was closed many years ago, and only recently opened again.

It had been a staple of the inn back in the day—a phone booth that patrons could use as needed by inserting coins into the coin slot and placing a call, obviously way before we had cellphones at the constant ready. A choice had been made to enclose it instead of ripping it out, because while it no longer made calls to the outside world, it did provide a line directly to the ghost who had resided here for centuries.

Earl, and I still wasn't sure if he was an actual Earl, as in an English lord type person, or if that just happened to be his name, had been here ever since he had tried to take my ancestor away with him. She had been promised to him in marriage. And then she hadn't shown up when she realized that to enter and live in his highfalutin world, she would have to give up anything and everything having to do with her powers. She had gotten off the boat that was moving her down toward her assigned fate and had made a different life for herself. But Earl had not been happy about being cheated of the beauty he'd been promised, so he'd come looking for her. And he'd met a fate of his own that he couldn't escape now.

He seemed to have made peace with it, though, and had even come back to rescue me the last time we were investigating a death. I appreciated that and him more than I could say, and tried not to bother him if he didn't want to be bothered. But I couldn't avoid it this time. I had to know if he'd been talking with Amelia. And I needed to ask him, as nicely, but as firmly as possible, to please cut off all communication until I had a chance to talk to her family.

I didn't have a lot of rules when it came to how other people led their lives, but I did when it came to how I led mine. I might have to lie to Dean by omission in not sharing how I got certain information and where I found it, but I was not going to lie to him about his own niece. Which meant I needed to sort this whole thing out before we went one step further down the road of finding out if Amelia truly was "of the blood" as my family called it, and if that meant she should be brought into the fold.

Putting all that aside, I entered the phone booth under the stairs and pulled the chain to light the bulb above my head. Once it was lit, I slowly closed the door and made sure it latched so that no light could be seen from the lobby. People sometimes wandered around in the night, and I had no problem with that, as long as they didn't hurt themselves or steal anything. Right now, though, I did not want to get caught talking into a payphone about ghosts and death when I had a full house. Well, minus that one, Walter, whom I should have put on my list and would as soon as I got this portion of the evening done.

Picking up the receiver, I dialed a number I'd been given many months ago. I didn't know if it actually was a connection or just a signal, and I hadn't wanted to ask when I'd first dealt with Earl. Maybe I should take the time to ask now if Amelia was talking with him. How had she known which numbers to push?

The phone rang and rang in my ear, and I was almost ready to hang up when Earl finally picked up.

"What can I do for you? Or should I say, what *more* can I do for you?"

Saucy, that was Earl, but I wasn't going to take him to task for that. He had done a lot for me, and I was incredibly grateful. But I needed him to do some more.

"I have a few questions. Do you want to do this over the phone, or do you want to meet out in the gazebo again? I don't really want to come down to the basement, to be honest."

"You scared of a little bit of clutter and spiderwebs?" He chuckled.

"No, of course not, and if there are a lot of spiderwebs, then I need to put the cleaning ladies on that. I found a bunch of dust in the library, and in one of the rooms, so maybe we need to do a spring-cleaning type thing if we've got dust and dirt everywhere."

He laughed this time. "I highly doubt you came to call regarding the cleaning habits of your employees. There seems to be another murder in the house, and I was wondering if you'd come to me for assistance."

"I was going to try not to because I didn't want to bother you if you had other things going on."

That got a big laugh this time. "What exactly do you think I'm doing down here? I don't have an appointment calendar and often drift around the area reminiscing to myself about things I'd done before or wishing for things I never took the chance to do. That takes up about twenty minutes out of every day. So, any time you need something, you just let me know because I'm pretty sure I'm available."

"I hadn't thought about that." I settled into the wooden bench and prepared myself for this conversation.

"Why would you? You have a ton of other things on your plate, my darling, and you do them well. Don't let that make your head too big, but it's true. Your Poobah was good at what he did, but he didn't have the finesse and the panache that you do. You're a quieter version of him, but a stronger one, and have far more control over things than he ever did. Don't forget that." I heard his hands clap and wondered how he did that when he was a ghost. "Now! Tell me why you're here, and what I can do for you. I'm at your service."

Where to start? Fortunately, I had brought one of my many lists with me and told him to hang on a second while I looked it over. "Okay, so first things first, did you see anything around the time of the death? She was killed this morning before breakfast with a candlestick in the library."

"Interesting way to go about the demise. I assume there were probably more lethal things to get the job done with, so I would think it was a crime of the moment instead of something that was plotted out well before it happened." He clicked his tongue. "I did not see anything or feel anything, except the passing of a soul. Although I feel that for anyone who is no longer with us in town, so I did not pay much attention to it. I did, however, notice that someone, or something, hung around for a few moments before noon this afternoon. I was embroiled in trying to figure out why I couldn't get the door to the former larder to open for me, since it often has before, but such is afterlife."

"So, nothing really different?" I jotted that down. "Did you get the door open? Do you want me to come down and do it for you?"

"As I said, not really anything different. I can look around, but I've been doing that since I heard about the murder through the floorboards below the library. So, I don't really have anything to add."

"Wait, you heard about the murder through the floorboards? Did you hear the murder?" I held my pencil poised above my pad, hoping for some laser-focused good information.

"I've been trying to remember if I heard anything, but I don't think I did. I was over in the wine cellar for a bit, and then I drifted that way to see why there were so many footsteps on the floor when I had thought everyone was leaving soon. That usually means more people at the lobby, not the library. Once I heard your voice, I left because I was positive you had everything in hand."

Being competent could bite you in the butt sometimes. "Well, if you think of anything, please let me know." I heaved out a sigh. "Now, I have to ask you about something, and I'm not mad or disappointed or scolding you, but I have to know."

He cleared his throat. "Well, that doesn't sound very good. Is Glennis giving you headaches again about that recipe card? I swear, I hear her reading the same words out over and over again, sometimes when I'm below the kitchen, as if she's sounding them out for the first time ever. I'm not sure what it does for her, but normally, she sounds almost hypnotic and dreamy when she gets to the last four. It's a bit bizarre, but since she never does more than recite them, I've never said anything."

"She recites them?"

"Almost on a daily basis. I haven't memorized them, since I tune her out as soon as she gets started, but it's very strange that it's a mix of common words that don't seem to go together. When she first did it years ago, I thought it might be a song, but it's very monotone, so I figured I was wrong and stopped listening."

I made another note to look through the words again on my phone. I so wished I could just ask Glennis, but I knew she wouldn't tell me. And if I could figure out what the deal was before, or at least have some idea of the significance before I approached her, I had a better chance of asking the right question the first time, instead of fumbling around and having her send me away.

"Is that the last question you had? Poobah tends to sneak into the exercise room first thing in the morning, and I like to set up little traps for him to see if I can keep him on his toes. He gets sad if he doesn't find something not in the right place when he comes in."

Oh, my word. But I wasn't going to stop their game as long as Poobah was safe. "Just don't let him be injured."

"Of course not."

"Okay then, back to my one more question before you go spread your shenanigans."

"Shoot."

"Have you been talking to the young girl who had that book last time? Her name is Amelia, and she sometimes comes into the phone booth when she can't sleep. I didn't think she was talking to anyone, but she just came to me today and told me that she's afraid she might have brought something into the house that she shouldn't have. I thought maybe she had just finally talked to you." The more I said, the more I hoped that he had talked to her, and that we weren't dealing with something more that I couldn't handle right now.

"Let me do some investigating of my own. I did not speak with this Amelia. I make a point to not answer unless I know it's you, which is why I gave you the number to reach me." He hummed for a moment as my heart fluttered in my chest. "Yes, I will look into this. I feel nothing out of the ordinary in the house, and I would be able to feel if there was something here that shouldn't be."

"That at least makes me feel a little better."

"Yes, I'm sure it does," he said absently. "I'll get back to you. I'll leave you a note in your room when I get any new information. I have to go."

"Okay, I'll wait to hear from you."

"As soon as possible." And then he hung up. I had meant to ask him about the memoir and how to get people to stop killing each other around here. Like, was there something in the house that hadn't been here before that was making people play out their murderous tendencies as they never had before? But he'd already gone, and I'd rather he be looking into if there was something in the house than getting his opinion on a memoir he probably knew nothing about.

I listened at the door for a moment to make sure there was no one in the lobby before opening up the space under the stairs. All was silent except for the ticking of the grandfather clock next to the coat rack across the way. If I could hear that, it meant no one else was out there.

The door squeaked when I pushed it open. It made me stop and look around as I tiptoed out. Still no one, so I released my breath and then closed the door gently behind me, making sure that it was fully latched. Now what? Suddenly, I was exhausted and wanted to go to bed. There were so many things I still wanted to look at and consider, but I also needed to go to bed. Tomorrow, or rather later today, since it was after midnight, was soon enough. I was going to be even more exhausted if I didn't give myself time to actually sleep.

I did, however, stop in the kitchen briefly to grab a couple of the cream puffs Glennis had made for tomorrow's breakfast. It was my inn. I didn't have to check with anyone. Then I walked down the hallway as quietly as possible. No one could probably hear me, since they were all upstairs, but I didn't want to take any chances that someone would see me and ask for something like a midnight snack.

So, sleep it was, while I tried to think about how to get people to talk to me about Glennis, and checked in with Dean to see if Isaac had found anything. Then I needed to see if I could get Glennis to talk with me, or maybe Poobah would spill the beans. Though he hadn't in all these years, so I had little hope tomorrow, or today rather, was going to be the day.

I was even more exhausted when I finally approached my door. Opening it, I walked right in and was not surprised at all to find Dean seated on my couch, flipping through the notes I'd left out and sipping a mug of hot chocolate.

"I was going to come out and look for you, but I was afraid you might be dealing with a guest issue, and I didn't want to interrupt. Everything okay?" He patted the couch next to him, lifting the corner of a blanket he had over his lap.

"It was just something I had to check on." Not a total lie, but I so hoped that someday soon I'd be able to talk to him about everything that was me instead of having to shield half of myself. I was good at it, I'd even made sure to not leave anything out, note-wise, that might have made him wonder what I was up to. I was careful about that in an effort to make sure that he never accidentally stumbled on anything. Of course, he could see the less traditional decorations and books around the room. But as with Aunt Hellen's talents as a séance leader, everyone thought it was just an interest, and because Dean had never pressed me on it, I had never tried to explain it.

Now I wondered if that had been a mistake on my part. Maybe if I had told him about my interest in these kinds of things and seen if he was okay with me not being like most normal people around here about religion, I could have told if that would have been a turn off.

And if my brain was going there right now, then I knew I was more tired than I thought I was.

"I'm glad you're back. I left Caper's house and had to tell Amelia to go back to bed and not come out again tonight when I walked by the gazebo. The child is eternally nocturnal, but with everyone still here, and a possible killer in the midst, we really want to keep her home."

"Of course. I told her the same thing earlier. I'm sorry she didn't listen."

His laugh was low, and I felt it through my head as I lay my cheek on his chest. "She hardly ever listens. We might need to fix that at some point, but right now, as long as she's safe, Caper is fine with her testing out her wings a little. He'll pull her back if things appear to be getting out of hand."

I closed my eyes as I rested there, wishing I could tell him that things might be far more out of hand than he realized, and we might have to pull those reins a little bit more firmly if she really did have talent and was of the blood. Why did this have to be so hard? If the council would just let us be out and about, then people would know there was magic, and you could make whatever choices rang with the way you wanted your life to go. I knew the precautions and the reasons. I'd been fine with them before because everyone had seemed okay with playing inside the rules that had been put down for very valid reasons, like not getting burned at the stake or being run out of town with pitchforks. But man, this was hitting hard and close to home. And yet, I wouldn't have chosen another person to do life with if he still wanted me after all was said and done.

"You've gone quiet. Should I let you rest? I was just going to check in to see if you were all right and not bother you if you were asleep. But then I saw your light on under the door and thought I'd see if you wanted some company."

"And then you stayed because you figured I was probably out getting a midnight snack, and I'd share with you?"

"Well, there was definitely some hope of that once I realized you were somewhere in the house because your car was still here."

Grabbing the small plate of cream puffs from the side table, I offered him first choice, which I didn't normally do for anyone else. We sat and talked about the investigation between bites, and I very gladly took the few minutes of calm before the storm I was going to have to brew tomorrow, later today, when I went out and talked to people who had known Glennis over the years. Isaac was still working on searching the web, so I provided the list I'd made of who was who and what they might have at stake with Penny's death.

And then we said goodnight at the door. His choice, not mine. He had to get up early for work and hadn't brought anything with him to spend the night. Plus, per his instructions, I was to get as much uninterrupted sleep as possible because he had this feeling in his gut that we were about to come into some big information from a few leads he had put out himself.

He wouldn't tell me what they were, or who they might be coming from, because he didn't want to be premature about what he might find. But we agreed to meet after his shift was done to go over what we had and start making some battle plans. I hoped that I would also have some more to share from Glennis.

I got that she had secrets, and I didn't want all of them. But there was something more going on here that she was not sharing, and it was making it very hard for me to get any real information that would send me in a different direction, while also clearing her name.

That was changing tomorrow, well, later today. Once I got some shut-eye and could see my way clear to letting my brain work on the puzzle that was Ms. Penny in the library with the candlestick.

Chapter 13

D awn came pretty early, especially since it had only been about five hours from when my head hit the pillow. First, I checked in with Glennis in the kitchen from my comfy nest of comforters and throws. She said she'd handle things, so I told her I was going back to sleep. Taking her at her word, I rolled over, knowing Aunt Hellen would be in shortly. And if all else failed, Poobah was probably on the grounds, working out after tripping over whatever Earl had deliberately messed up in the exercise room.

Two hours later, I woke up in my comfy bed and stared at the ceiling for a few minutes. This was my life, and even with the murders and the hindrance from being able to give myself completely to Dean, I loved it. I had the hotel I'd dreamed of for years, friends, and more importantly, family who I loved more than anything else in the world. Dean and his little motley crew fell into that friend group, until maybe we could change that to family.

I was not going to get ahead of myself just yet, though. I had a lot to do before I could seriously consider testing out how he'd feel about someone who wasn't just interested in things outside the norm, but actually practiced them.

After quickly changing into jeans and a sweatshirt, I headed out to pound the pavement about Glennis. Of course, I couldn't really tell the people I planned on talking to that was my goal, but I'd look much more likely to not be sleuthing if I just happened to be walking by their house or establishment and popped in to say hi in my casual clothes instead of being dressed up for the inn.

Time and walking would tell if it worked. But at least I was comfortable and not trying to hoof it all over town in my heels. I adored those things, but they made no sense for how many steps I was anticipating.

First up was Mrs. Lincoln. She knew everyone and everything that went on around town. Plus, she'd been here for a lot of years. She was also one of Norm's least favorite people, and that could definitely work in my favor.

As I approached her small house on the waterfront of the Susquehanna River, I tried to think of how to approach her. Yes, I thought that her detesting Norm, the lead cop, could work in my favor, but she also wasn't very friendly to anyone. In fact, she called the cops on squirrels that irritated her, so this could go a couple of ways. I hoped it went well, but I was braced for it also being a certain sort of chaos.

She had a beautiful fence running around the entirety of her property. It kept the maniacal dog she had away from everyone. But, even though her car was in the driveway to the left, she didn't answer the door when I continuously knocked.

Finally, Roger, next door, came out and waved to me. "She took her dog on a vacation to the Jersey Shore. Quietest few days I've ever had, and I'm not ashamed to admit that."

"Ha! No doubt." Darn it. So much for starting off right!

"Don't tell her I said that."

"Of course not. You'd never hear the end of it."

"Oh, it would be much worse than that."

I started to laugh, but he looked way too serious, so I cut myself off. "I promise I will not say a word to her about anything. I rarely talk to her anyway."

"Lucky you." He finally smiled. "Is there something I can help you with? I might not be able to give you all the current gossip. Usually, she rambles on about it to her dog in the back yard, and I'm up to date, but with her gone, I've heard nothing. Not even the incessant barking. That thing is a menace, and I love dogs, but he does provide me with all kinds of information while I'm sitting in my back yard reading my books."

A guy after my own heart, even if he was old enough to be my grandfather. And with him, I probably didn't have to beat around the bushes shielding his backyard from Mrs. Lincoln's.

"Here's the deal." I took a deep breath. "I'm looking into the murder that happened at the inn. Glennis is being targeted as a suspect due to something found with the body, and her nephew is bound and determined to get someone for the crime. I believe that he thinks he's doing the right thing."

Roger rolled his eyes at that, and I couldn't agree more with him, but I didn't want to get off topic.

"So, he's trying to make something stick to someone, and I need to make sure it's not Glennis. If she were the real culprit, I'd hand her over, if necessary, but I just know she didn't do it. I need proof, though, and I thought it might help if I knew more about her when she was younger."

This was, of course, mostly true. I would admit only to myself that I also had some hope of maybe brushing up against what she might have on Poobah that made her have a free get-out-of-anything card.

"Glennis." He tapped a bony finger to his chin. "Well, I know that she was a spitfire when she was younger." He chuckled. "She's still a spitfire in many ways, but back in her early twenties, she was involved with someone that she thought she'd marry, and it didn't happen. I don't remember why. Sorry. But it was a long time ago. Other than that, after he went away, she seemed to buckle down and got the job at the inn and has been there ever since. So, a spitfire, but a far less adventurous one. Not sure if that helps. But other than that, I'm not sure what to tell you."

"No, that definitely helps, thank you, Roger. Any time you want to come up for breakfast, you just let me know. And we'll put out a spread for you. Maybe give me a couple of weeks. since a lot of people are leaving for vacation. But after that, we'll get you whatever you want."

"Yeah, I heard you were giving everyone the time off. That's nice of you, but I hear it will also benefit you since you're cozying up to that ferry guy. Dean, right? I've seen his family around town. They seem like upstanding citizens, and I always appreciate seeing a family reunited."

Upstanding might have been too generous a word for what life Caper had led before he'd settled into the cottage, but I certainly wasn't going to tell Roger that. I thanked him again and wandered off.

"Hey!" he yelled when I was halfway down the sidewalk.

I turned around and he came down his porch steps to meet me halfway, right in front of Mrs. Lincoln's house. It seemed so weird to not have all conversations drowned out by ferocious barking from a tiny dog.

"You might want to drop in on Chessie Franks. She and Glennis ran together for some years. I think she was going to be her maid of honor, so she might have something that will give you more background."

Interesting! "Seriously, anything you want for breakfast. Let me know, and it's yours."

He patted me on the shoulder, then turned toward his quiet house.

I headed back up the hill from the ferry launch at the end of the street, waving to Dean as I walked by his post. He was knee deep, literally, in the river, working on something along the port side of the ferry. I'd ask him about it later. Right now, I had one Chessie Franks to hunt down and get some answers from, if she'd talk to me.

It wasn't that she didn't like to talk. She loved to talk about anything and everything, especially if you were sitting in her chair at the beauty salon on Main. The problem was that I hadn't sat in her chair in quite some time. And she was probably going to give me grief for abandoning her, especially when she'd be able to tell that I was still getting my short hair cut somewhere, just not here.

I sighed and girded my loins because it had to be done. Like dealing with customers at the inn when they were being a problem, I'd just settle in, let her say her piece, and then ask for what I wanted. I'd survive, probably barely. But I'd survive.

I found her sitting out front at her shop on a bench, people watching and smiling.

"Hey Chessie! Not too booked up today?"

"That means I could fix what you've done to your hair now and also tackle those eyebrows. Child, you have got to do better if you want to be taken seriously as a proprietor of your fine establishment." She flicked her gaze over me from top to bottom. "Though I have been hearing that you've got some issues with people coming in, but not making it out alive." The raised, perfectly sculpted eyebrow was the final knife in the gut I did not need.

"Always a pleasure to see you, Chessie."

"You know it."

"I do. And I promise to come see you for a spruce up,"

"You'd better." She let her gaze roam over my hair and face again.

I did everything I could to keep my hands down at my side. Because I very much wanted to shield my haircut from her laser focus and harsh judgment.

"Even your boyfriend comes here, and I enjoy seeing him walk up every time. Very fine specimen there, I'll tell you."

On that, at least, we agreed.

"I'll let him know he brings joy to your day."

She cackled and then poked me in the arm as she stood up. "No matter how much I wish you'd let me handle that hair and those eyebrows, I'm aware that you are probably not here for that since you haven't come by in a while." There went the cocked eyebrow again. "So, then, what can I do for you, Miss Roxy Gleason? You have another murder case on your hands, which makes me assume that you need information. I can tell you your victim was a bit cagey in many ways. This was supposed to be a family vacation, and the whole passel of those people were constantly on the move throughout town, but there were more than a few times I saw the matriarch shy off from the crowd and go do her own thing. All the ladies and girls were to come in for the spa works, while the men were over at the art gallery getting ready for some kind of show, and yet she left in the middle of the event. Saying she got a text or something, but she never actually looked at her phone. I watch for these things."

"Of course, you do." And I was so thankful she did.

"You're darn right I do. Have to know whether someone is about to skip out on the bill. But she paid in full, with a very nice tip, I can tell you that, before leaving the premises, and she did not return. Those ladies waited here for about thirty minutes after they were done, wandering around, each of them texting her and asking where she was, but no one was getting an answer. Then out of nowhere, she comes breezing in, looking like she had a little bed head, if you get my meaning, and they all took off. She refused to answer any questions."

I got her meaning and remembered that Leon had felt she had someone on the side that needed to be looked into. Were they the person on the nanny cam that had been caught? I put that on my mental list and hoped I remembered to ask, along with my thousand other questions. But I had a witness, here and now, and had to focus on what Chessie was telling me, so I didn't miss anything. "As in, she said no to any questions, or that they weren't allowed to ask her?"

Chessie tilted her head and looked up at the sky. "No, it was more like she just skated over it masterfully and redirected every single time. You could see the frustration on the daughters' faces, but then they all deflated and yielded to her when she walked out the door, telling them they could follow her or not. She had things to do."

"And they went on to the art gallery?" That was going to have to be my next stop, then. Follow the trail.

"No, then they all went to lunch, and Mavis over there came in after to drop the intel on me, since that's what we do. You should come by sometime. You might learn a thing or two. I'd tell you if you were in the chair."

"Come on, Chessie."

She chuckled and poked me again. "Okay, I'll stop, and your hair isn't really that bad. But it does look like you might have taken the scissors to your bangs on your own, which I know you know not to do."

I couldn't stop the blush that flared up my neck. I had used the scissors in the bathroom this morning to cut a bit of the left side because it wasn't lining up correctly. Maybe I wasn't the only one who could "see" things even if a person didn't want to tell me.

"Ah, well, don't touch the eyebrows. I'll do them for you next week, totally at my expense, simply because I want you to look your best. Something is going to happen soon, I can feel it in my gut, and you're going to want to look your best, too."

I smoothed a finger over the left eyebrow and then got back to the real reason I was here. "I'll take you up on your offer, but I can pay for it. Did Mavis have anything that seemed to point to where Penny had gone or how often that happened?"

She shrugged. "Pretty much every time they went out. But Mavis said that once Penny shut down a conversation, it was shut down, and since she was the one who handed over the credit card every time, they didn't push too much."

"Okay, thanks." I bit my lip. "Now, I appreciate the info on Penny, but I also wanted to see if you know anything about Glennis."

Chessie narrowed her eyes. "She works for you. Why don't you know all the things about Glennis?"

A few people came out onto the sidewalk from across the street. We had stood out here too long, and people were starting to wonder about our conversation. I did not want that.

"Tell you what, why don't you wax my eyebrows now? If you have time, that is."

"I absolutely do." Smiling mischievously, she opened the glass door for me, then waved to everyone who had come out to be nosy. I wasn't surprised when they all went back into their businesses and homes. Most likely, they knew that she'd spill the gossip as soon as I left. I just had to make sure that what she was spilling could work in my favor.

She didn't have to direct me to the chair, since I knew where it was, and that this was going to freaking hurt. But my tweezers had not been up to snuff in quite some time. As always, I would love the end result, but I was going to wince and probably leak tears as the process happened.

Because she wasn't doing my hair, I didn't need the cape. I settled in with my neck positioned on the wash bowl and closed my eyes. I could do this.

The wax was warm when she smoothed it over the top arch of my left brow. I braced myself as she patted a small piece of cloth over the wax and used her finger to swipe back and forth to adhere it to the wax.

I blew out a breath.

"It's not that bad, and you know it. Even if it's been quite some time since we've done this, it's not worth bracing yourself like that."

She was probably talking about the way I had my fingers curled around the armrests and my fingertips dug into the underside. Or maybe the way I had my eyes screwed shut.

"You are very much aware that I cannot pull the strips if your whole face is crinkled." She sighed. "All right, talk to me. What do you need to know?"

I opened my eyes and looked up at her.

And she yanked the strip. Hard.

"Nice!" she said, feathering her finger over the brow that was left and admiring her handiwork. "Now talk."

"That actually wasn't as bad as I remember."

"It never was, but every time you seem to forget that until after I pull the first one." She smiled. "Now, talk."

"I know that everyone is going to ask you what we talked about, and I want to make sure that whatever you tell them doesn't make me look like an idiot."

"Oh, sugar, I'd never do that to you." She dipped a new application stick into the pot of hot wax and twirled it, so the strands broke. Using her fabulous skills, she painted that wax under the arch of the same brow.

"Okay, I'm going to hold you to that, Chessie."

She cackled as she ripped off the next strip. It wasn't as bad this time.

I continued through the slight pain. "So, you told me about the people who are staying at the inn, but Glennis's nephew is really looking into her for this murder, and I can't figure out why. Do you have any insight on why a recipe card would incite someone to kill another person?"

"Recipe card?" She halted as she drew in a sharp breath.

I opened my eyes to look at her and caught her widened eyes before she forcefully relaxed her face into a joking smile. It felt off because it was off.

"Please don't tell me any big lies. I'd rather you tell me you don't know what I'm talking about than try to spin some story that will send me off in a direction that's really not going to help."

Leaning back against the wash bowl at the chair next to me, Chessie pinched the bridge of her nose. "No one talks about this."

"I'm not surprised about that. Something happened a lot of years ago, and it's put a chokehold on Poobah, and by extension, me, with Glennis. I don't know what it is, and personally, I would let it slide, but if it has anything to do with the recipe being found under the murder victim's chair, then I'm not getting anywhere without that information, and neither are the police."

"There was an unexpected death a lot of years ago."

Chapter 14

I had to tread carefully here because the woman who would normally tell you anything and everything in a bright and cheery voice had dropped that voice an octave and seemed to have pulled in on herself. I didn't want to frighten her, and I felt horrible that she appeared to shrink down with that one sentence, but I needed more. If only to understand what had happened all those years ago, and how it had anything to do with the death of a woman none of us had ever met, that I knew of.

"Please don't stop there. There was a death? When? Who was it?"

Turning to the counter with the wax warmer, she very carefully and deliberately put the application stick down on the sea green expanse, and then braced her hands on the curved edge.

"I'm not sure I should be talking about this. It was a very long time ago and brings up pain that many people might not have completely dealt with, even after all this time."

That sounded very serious. Of course, any death would cause grief, but this seemed to have deeper layers, and no one talked about it. I had never heard of anything from thirty years ago.

"Can you tell me something? Anything at all? You don't have to give me all the details. But if I at least had something to jump off with on the internet search, then I might be able to follow the trail all on my own, without bringing it to anyone's attention."

She bit her lip and tapped her long fingernails on the counter. Shaking her head so that her curly hair sprang left and right, she closed her eyes and sighed. "Let me finish your eyebrows while I think about what I want to say, and then I'll tell you some, but I only know some. And I would be very careful about asking anyone about this. You do your research on the internet, or whatever, but I wouldn't go around asking about it. You're going to stir up some people that you do not want to stir up."

I lay my head back down and let her do the next two strips on my other eyebrow. She took the tweezers and cleaned up the rest, then smoothed some soothing lotion over the places she'd waxed.

Normally, she would have held up a mirror for me to see her handiwork, but as soon as she was done, she turned away to pace.

"I was going to be a bridesmaid at the Justice of the Peace. I thought I'd be the maid of honor, but that didn't pan out when she chose someone else. And then the whole thing didn't happen because Anthony Fromm died in a boating accident on the river, and that was the end of that." Tapping her fist on the wall, she looked back at me, finally. "Most of us were left completely in the dark about what exactly had happened, but that recipe was supposed to be for the wedding breakfast that Glennis was going to make to celebrate the day after."

"Oh, no."

"Oh, yeah. I don't know what your grandfather's part is in all of it, but for a while she only did her job in the kitchen, and then went home and cried and slept, sometimes at the same time. Eventually, she emerged from her enforced solitude. We'd checked in on her, but Poobah would tell us he'd relay our messages to her because she wasn't taking any visitors at the time. When she did come out, she didn't want to talk about it, and she looked relatively happy, so we kept our questions to ourselves. Then we all kind of drifted away from each other, and with each year, and then each decade that passed, it seemed to fade from memory. I don't know why it's back now, but if you find anything out, I want you to tell me. I need closure, Roxy. I didn't realize how much I needed closure until you just brought this up, and it hit me like a basket of sopping wet towels."

That image would stay with me for some time. "Do you know if she stayed in the hotel when she was in her hermit days?"

"No, she was in that cottage you have at the back of the property."

I was stunned into immobility, and also absolutely raring to go do some more hands-on sleuthing. But I didn't want to leave while Chessie still seemed to be caught back in a time thirty years ago.

"I'm sorry I had to bring all this up. I would have made more of an effort not to be so forceful if I had known what I was asking."

"It's okay. Like I said, I wasn't expecting it to hit me so hard. I can't even imagine what Glennis must be going through if someone took that recipe card and upset her apple cart. Should I call her?"

I gave myself a moment to consider the ramifications there. "I don't think so. I have no idea what people outside the police and the people who were in the library when she was found know, and I don't want to get in trouble for sharing things I shouldn't have. I will keep you updated, though, on anything I find out. I'm sorry for bringing your pain back up, Chessie. I really had no idea."

"Maybe it's just time." She gave a low chuckle. "I'll listen to whatever you have to say if you let me handle those bangs for you."

I got out of the chair and took her in for a big hug. She hesitated for a second to put her arms around my waist, but when she did, she gave me a huge squeeze.

"Go do your thing."

"What do I owe you?" I asked.

"Pshh. Just some answers and a crack at getting you back in the chair."

"Deal." As I left out the front door, I barely kept myself from waving to all the people standing in their front windows while I strolled along the sidewalk. I had a feeling Chessie's phone was going to be blowing up any second now. As for me, I had work to do. First and foremost, I was going to visit the cottage where a grieving Glennis had spent a whole lot of time and might have left something behind that no one had thought to check into. The décor, the furniture, and the books had never changed in the space. Poobah had kept it the same for the last fifty years after my grandmother had decorated it for them. I hadn't changed anything, either, when I took over owning the property and the inn. Some things had probably been moved around when Caper and his kids had moved in, but it would all still be there. I just needed to get my hands on some of those books.

It wasn't yet lunch time, even though my feet and I were pretty sure it had to be at least ten o'clock at night. I had one more stop to make before I could go curl up on my couch and digest what I'd heard, as well as make a plan on what to look up on the internet. This one, I was probably not going to be able to give to Isaac. I didn't want to explain why I needed it until I had more information.

But first, the cottage.

I let myself into the backyard through the gate near our small garden shed. Running my hand over the hydrangea bush that bordered the building, I worked on what I would say about wanting to put my hands all over all the things in the house.

Maybe I'd just say I was looking for a particular book and hope that something would throw out a sparkle. Though that would mean Dean might hear that hum, and possibly Amelia would see the glow.

I couldn't worry about that right now. I had to get in the door first.

When I knocked, Caper whipped the door open, as if I might be the cops. Although that wouldn't be too far off, with the way he had previously lived his life.

"Oh, hey, Hottie! Dean's not here. He took the kids out for some shopping that apparently I am not allowed to take part in because it's for my birthday."

Hottie, that was the way Dean had me listed in his phone, and Caper had never really called me anything else. I smiled at him. "When is your birthday?" My mind was running through whether I could talk Glennis into making him a cake. I probably could. She liked him, and Dean, and the kids far more than she seemed to like me sometimes.

That wasn't entirely fair. Glennis liked me just fine and could be very nice. Now was just a slice of time where things were wonky.

My mind then flipped over to the fact that everyone who might have seen or heard something was out of the house!

"I'm looking for a particular book, and Poobah thought it might be over here."

Caper opened the door wider and swept his hand out as he bowed. "Your house, so whatever you need, go ahead and take it."

"It's your house, too," I said.

He chuckled. "I knew you were going to say that, but since I haven't even paid any rent up to this point, and you're making it very easy for us to stay, I'm going to say it's very much your house."

"You've done a bunch of projects around here. That's enough." I walked past him. That conversation was over. Heading for the bookcase in the living room, I really hoped whatever I needed was there. Other cases were peppered around the house in each of the three bedrooms, but I didn't want to have to step into the private areas of other people. Except I really needed that book, whichever one it was.

I would have also liked to look through the house and see if there were any random hidey-holes that maybe Glennis had stashed something in. But she probably would have come back in here at some point over the years to retrieve it.

So, the book it was. Now to find it.

Caper and I split off in the front room as I headed to the left, where the bookcase was, and Caper headed to the right, entering the kitchen. Good, I would feel more comfortable looking around for that sparkle without an audience.

As I ran my gaze over the bookcase, I didn't see anything that caught my eye. I ran my finger over every book spine, hoping that something would light up for me so that I could grab it and get out of here.

"You want something to drink?" Caper called from the kitchen, peeking his head around the corner.

I straightened immediately and shoved my hands behind my back.

The quirk of his brow made me think that was a very bad move. I was up against someone who knew all the tricks and had used them throughout the many years where he'd skated the line between legal and illegal shenanigans.

He grinned, though, and walked backward into the kitchen. "There isn't anything in the house that you'd want to steal, since almost all of it is yours, and the rest is probably dusty or dirty. The good stuff is either in a safe, or I gave it back to those I shouldn't have taken it from in the first place." He chuckled from the other room, and the sound ghosted around the furniture.

I was about to just grab a book and run when I finally saw a tiny little glow on a low shelf. There was a big teddy bear resting against the case, and that's how I had missed it in the first place. To better cover my tracks this time, I bent down and ran my hands over the few books before the one I wanted, and then scooched the teddy bear out of the way to reach for the one I wanted.

It burst into a rainbow of colors the second I touched it, and all I wanted to do was leave so I could open the book and let it tell me all its secrets.

Rising, I turned and found myself face to face with Caper. I had not heard him come up behind me. Although, to be fair to myself, he had been a cat burglar in days gone by, so he was probably used to not making a sound.

"Oh," I said, dropping back a step.

"I do want to sincerely thank you for everything you've done for us, Roxy. I was not in the best of places, and now I am, and so are my kids. I know Amelia keeps sneaking away to some place within the inn, and I hope she's not bothering you."

I couldn't help but smile. "She's never bothered me. Honestly, she is one of the most delightful people I've ever met, and I've met a lot of people."

He kicked his toe into the area rug that had been in the same place for decades. "She can be a lot to handle sometimes."

"And yet you're doing an amazing job. We're also all here to help in any way we can. If you need a break, send her to me or Aunt Hellen. I swear to you, sometimes I think I've been replaced as the favorite niece, and I find myself not minding at all."

He glanced up at me, and I was surprised to see there was a glistening sheen to his eyes. His gaze went back to the carpet. "You have no idea how much that means to me. To us." He cleared his throat. "Now, we need to talk about a few things. I see you found your book."

I held it up for him to see the fruits of my labor and was then immediately horrified that I did. Nothing like holding out a copy of *Seducing Your Mate to Mate*. It hadn't exactly been a bestseller back in the day, and probably wouldn't be now, but I had to come up with a reason as to why I'd had to have this and fast.

He chuckled. "You aren't going to have to do much convincing, in case you're wondering. I haven't had a conversation that didn't have your name in it, in glowing terms, for months now. I think I've been replaced as the person Dean loves the most, and I find myself not minding at all."

"I see what you did there."

"I wasn't trying to hide it. And I'm thrilled, honestly. Dean deserves much more than he thinks, and if you're the one to show him that, then I am totally here for it. Just don't try to rope him into any of those traditional wedding things if he ever gets up the courage to ask you. And don't expect some huge spectacle when he asks. He's much more low-key than that, but I think you already are aware."

The thought of marriage made my insides tingle, both in anticipation and dread. I couldn't say yes if I couldn't be all of myself with him. And I couldn't give up my place in my world and this world to be with him. I very firmly kept my smile in place. In this, at least, I was the master at keeping things close to the vest. I'd done it my whole life after all.

"You said a few things?" I asked to redirect the conversation.

"Yes, speaking of hiding things. Dean mentioned this morning that you were going to look into this murder thing because Glennis says she didn't do it, but her nephew isn't sure."

"True. I need to know who the real killer is, and I'm not sure that Norm can handle these kinds of investigations. This is the third, and he wouldn't have had the culprit in the first two if it hadn't been for this meddling kid."

"Scooby Doo, I see what you did there."

"I wasn't trying to hide it."

"Touché. But there is someone who was trying to hide things. From the beginning of this family's stay, I saw Penny outside in the gazebo. I thought at first she was reading by the lights you have installed in the roof, but then I realized she was looking at her phone. When it lit up the first night and she left, I wasn't sure if it was someone texting her or maybe an alarm that she set for herself. Some people need that device for pretty much everything."

"Don't even get me started on that. We'll be here for hours."

"I'll take a rain check, since I expect the family to be back in about thirty minutes, and I was hoping to get some straightening up done around here without everyone underfoot." He put his hands on his slim hips. "The thing is that the second night, she was out there again, and again, she was looking at her phone. The screen flashed, reflecting off her glasses, and she got up and went into the house. I wasn't exactly watching what she was doing, per se, because I was waiting for Amelia to come back from a jaunt to Glennis's treat cabinet before we could do movie night. But I did see a light on the third-floor flash on and a couple standing in the window in a pretty tight embrace before they drew the curtains."

Third floor? But that was where Walter had been staying, and no one else...

"So, then I made sure to look out again on the next night, and the exact same ritual happened. Except it wasn't the phone that sent her up, it was the light in the window. As soon as she saw it turn on, she nearly ran out of the gazebo. I don't know who was on the third floor, but I'm pretty certain that Penny might have been wishing that she had that book you've got in your hands. I never saw her with anyone but her family throughout the day, yet I saw her every night with the guy on the third floor."

"Thank you. I'm going to follow that trail and see where it leads. That could be really helpful. Seriously, thanks!"

"You've already wandered off in your mind to all the ways this could be connected with everything else, so I'm going to let you go with your book. I won't tell Dean, but there might be a cost down the road." He cracked a half smile at me.

"Ha! Yes, well, thanks again, and when the time comes, I'll have you negotiate with Mena. She's my representative in all things having to do with brokering deals."

"I don't doubt it." He laughed, and I left before Dean and the kids got home, so I didn't get caught up in more conversation when I had a book to pilfer for information.

Of course, I wanted to know what they got Caper for his birthday, which meant I'd make a point to ask later. I loved checking in with them, plus I would need to talk with Dean after I went through and got whatever this book's message was. But first, I had to get the message, and to do that, it was best if I were alone.

I entered the inn through the double doors off the dining room and then quick-stepped my way down the hall with the book under my arm. If I could make it past Aunt Hellen and the kitchen without drawing attention, then I should be able to make it to my room without any incidents.

The coast was clear, which was a little strange, since it was right before lunch. I would have expected people to be milling around in the lobby, getting ready to eat whatever Glennis had conjured up for their meal. Maybe they were all in their rooms?

But as I stayed close to the wall to avoid detection while heading to my rooms, I heard a lot of laughter coming out of the billiard room. Maybe they were all in there playing darts and shooting pool. I would text Aunt Hellen when I closed the door behind me to let her know where to find them all when Glennis, Clara, and Taylor laid out lunch.

Doing my duties in both realms could be overwhelming, but I had yet to falter, and I wasn't going to start now.

I softly closed the door behind me and then breathed a sigh of relief when no one was in here to greet me. I'd had Mena let herself in a time or two, and Dean also. Aunt Hellen rarely showed up here without letting me know ahead of time she was coming my way. Same with Poobah. And none of them tried to contact me, so I was in the clear.

All right then. Time to get down to business.

I set out my candles and my talismans, backed myself up into the nest of pillows I kept on the bed, and then sat cross-legged in the mattress with my eyes closed.

"Please show me what I need to know here. What message are you carrying that I need to solve this travesty?" I asked, my hand firmly on the cover of the book.

I flipped it open about a quarter of the way through the pages, still with my eyes shut. I blew out the breath I'd been holding, and lights shot out from the book, glowing bright enough for me to know the colors were there even through my closed eyes.

And when I opened them, the light show was even more spectacular than I had imagined it could be. It was like a mini fireworks show that the town put on at the riverfront on the Fourth of July. Every color of the rainbow was represented, and even some that I wouldn't know the name of. They flew left and right, and I almost worried for a second that they could possibly set my comforter on fire. But they didn't. They fizzled out an inch above the fabric, just as another colorful display shot out of the book. I was not going to be able to read the words on the page if this thing didn't simmer down. At the last second, I remembered saying something to that effect when this phenomenon had first started, and how the lights had shut themselves down, like I had scolded them, and they were taking their toys and going home.

I didn't say anything this time, but I did lay my hand on the place where the pages were secured in the middle of the book and then waited.

After a few seconds, the colors stopped, and a steady, mellow gold glow pulsed from the pages. It rippled under the black letters on the beige, thick paper the text had been printed on, as if something underwater was swimming along under the text, just waiting to surface.

The tension was killing me, but I stayed patient, even though that tended to be contrary to my inner core's purpose.

And then a series of letters formed from the golden glow, coalescing into words. I wasn't sure what I had wanted it to say, but I wasn't expecting it to be so pointed.

Find the ghost of love and ask the question.

Chapter 15

"**W**hat in the heck does that mean?" I asked.

The book remained silent.

"Is there anything else I need to do?"

Still nothing.

"Can you tell me anything about this guy who was linked to Glennis that died?"

Yet, again, absolutely nothing.

I dropped the book into my lap and crossed my arms over my chest. I wasn't afraid to admit that I was a bit irritated by the vague answer and then nothing else. With all the fireworks and hoopla, I really thought the answer would have been far more specific.

Who the heck was the ghost of love, and what questions was I supposed to ask? I felt less in the know after the message than I had before, and that was not a good place to be. I couldn't even go to Dean with anything concrete without finding this ghost first and asking whatever question I had to ask.

I flopped back into my pillow nest and gave myself about thirty seconds to have a little tantrum by grumbling at the ceiling, and then it was time to get to work. I put the candles and the talismans away, and then straightened the bedspread. I put the book in the drawer of my nightstand because I did not want

Dean to walk in and see the title. His brother might tell him, anyway, but I could say someone had requested the book, and I'd handed it off. I couldn't do that if he saw it sitting on my coffee table. I wasn't a fan of lying to him, but at least this one would be a little white lie/fib-type thing. That I could handle.

I was going to have to go down into the cellar and hope that I could get Earl to meet me there without a phone call at midnight. Most likely, I could have asked Aunt Hellen to hold a séance or something to call in the ghost of love, but I had a feeling in my gut that doing that could set off a chain of events I wasn't ready to handle. We'd go the easy way first.

I headed back out from my room and went past the quiet billiards room. Aunt Hellen must have grabbed the family and herded them into the dining room for lunch. Good for her, and that meant I shouldn't have to interact with any of the guests on my way down to the cellar.

But that didn't mean I wasn't going to be halted in my Love Ghost quest by my aunt herself.

"Oh, look at your beautiful eyebrows!" She came out from behind the counter and put her hand under my chin, then turned my head left and right. "Chessie?"

She chuckled when I rolled my eyes under my perfect brows. "Did she call you and tell on me?"

"No, not at all. Now, where are you sneaking off to?"

I didn't trust that she and Chessie hadn't been on the phone two seconds after I closed the door on the woman's shop behind me. Not at all. But I had more important things to do than to pin my aunt down on her fibs.

Stepping in closer, I dropped my voice, just in case anyone was around that I didn't want to overhear our conversation. "I got a message from the books finally."

"Oh, that's wonderful. What was said?"

I gave her the rundown on the teddy thing, and what that might reference, and also the Love Ghost thing. "Do you have any idea of what a Ghost of Love could be?"

She shook her head. "It's not ringing any bells, and I hesitate to try to call anything by that name to me, as it could mean a bunch of different things."

"Yeah, I thought about a séance, but with people in the house, and with so many uncertainties, I'm not willing to risk it."

"I completely agree. So, you're going to talk to Earl then, I assume?"

"Yes, he had said that he only has about twenty minutes of his day taken up with his regular routine, so I could talk to him whenever, and ask him for help with whatever. I appreciate that, of course, but I don't want to bother him."

"Earl needs to be bothered. I think we all left him alone for far too long. He needs interaction, and if he's asking for it from you, then please take him up on the offer."

This was probably a good time to let her know about Amelia's concerns, but the door to the dining room swung open and Leon stalked out with storm clouds on his face. Aunt Hellen shooed me away and put on her best smile. I took her up on the free pass this time, knowing I might have to pay for it later, but such was the business of owning an inn.

The door to the cellar was off the foyer, and not a place anyone was allowed to go without an escort from the staff. Even then, I didn't like people down there. It was a warren of rooms that began with a wine cellar housing many different flavors and vintages of wine. We didn't need everyone to know what exactly we had down here. Besides, now that I knew Earl was a resident of the area, I hesitated to send anyone into the space unattended, just in case.

Beyond the wine room, there were also several storage areas I didn't often visit. Then, a few months ago, I also found a room stocked with furniture and memorabilia from all of the lives that had been lived in this place, dating back to when it first opened. I hadn't had a ton of time to go through everything, but Dean and I had put it on our list of staycation forays. I was itching to dive in, just as soon as I figured out who the murderer was, and could send everyone, but Earl, on vacation.

Descending the stairs into the cellar, I kept my hand on the railing. They were incredibly narrow, so I kind of side-stepped my way down each tread and kept my head ducked, so as not to smack anything important on the low ceiling. Wouldn't want to pull the focus away from my newly done eyebrows with a bruise or two...

Finally, I made it to the bottom and flipped the lights on in the wine cellar. Hundreds of bottles of wine, some over a hundred years old, lined the walls and rested in racks in the middle of the floor. They were handmade by Poobah when he and my grandmother, whom we had affectionately called Grand Duchess before she passed away, were traveling the world. They'd spent a lot of time picking up bottles with no intent on drinking themselves, but not wanting to leave each country without something.

We had many guests order these bottles to be sent up to their rooms, or they bought them for special occasions, like anniversaries. We rarely used them when we hosted weddings, since no one wanted to pay for vintage wine for over a hundred people.

I went around the racks and opened the door to the next room. I didn't want to try to talk to Earl out in the open, just in case someone like Mena or Aunt Hellen came down. They would not be shocked by me talking to the ghost, but it would interrupt the conversation I was hoping to have with Earl. I was afraid that might throw me off whatever trail I thought I was going to be on about this new ghost I was supposed to find.

What the heck was a Ghost of Love? I hoped I was about to find out.

"Earl? Earl, can you come out, please? I don't have time to wait to call you tonight, and you did say that I could call you whenever I needed something."

I had never really called him like this, so I wasn't certain what to expect. I looked around to see if he would come through a wall or sink down through the ceiling. Nothing happened.

"Earl?"

"Right behind you." He sounded weary, and I wasn't sure why, or if I was supposed to ask.

I decided I didn't care what the normal rules were. "Are you okay? You look worn, my friend."

The way his eyes widened, and then how he turned his head, made me wonder if I'd said the wrong thing.

"Your friend?"

"I'm sorry, am I not supposed to think of you as a friend? Is that an otherworldly kind of thing?"

He shook his head before looking at me again. "I don't think anyone has called me that in a very long time." He rested an elbow on the rack of very pricey wines. "We're not here to listen to me go on about that kind of thing. I had made my bed all those years ago. I was not a person that someone would call a friend. That was the path I chose willingly. What is it that you need?"

Squinting at him, I left the question and the pause hanging in the air. "We'll table the discussion for now, but don't expect to get out of it next time."

"So noted. Your question?

"Funny you should ask it that way. I finally got some sparkles from a book, and the message was to find the Ghost of Love and ask my question. You wouldn't happen to be the Ghost of Love, would you?"

That got him to laugh from his belly, and it was a wonderful sound, even in the midst of all this uncertainty.

"No, I can very much assure you I am not this Ghost of Love you've been tasked with finding." He cocked his head to the side. "Was that the exact phrasing that your book gave you?"

"Verbatim."

"Hmmm, this requires some outside assistance, perhaps. Or maybe a convening with another entity."

I wrinkled my new eyebrows. "I'd rather not have Aunt Hellen do a séance, if I can avoid it. There are too many people here, and since the person who died is one of their relatives, I'm afraid they'll ask for her to be pulled back, and I don't think that's how my aunt works. Plus, not everyone is okay with that kind of stuff." A lot of people gave a side-eye to the woo-woo stuff, anyway. Unless it was on TV, then all bets were off. But seeing it in real life, directly in front of you, could scare even me, and I knew what was going on.

"There is a possibility..."

I didn't jump in to ask what that possibility was when he trailed off. I watched as he paced two inches above the floor from one side of the wine cellar to the other and back. Patience was definitely not my virtue, but I was going to put off stomping my foot on the ground and begging for answers for as long as I could.

He turned at the farthest point from me. "There is a way. I haven't used the method in many years, as I had no need or desire to interact with anyone beyond myself. Horribly quaint for a hermit, but there you have it."

I motioned for him to continue, and he just smiled.

"Let me tell my story. You won't be able to run and do what I'm proposing at this moment, anyway, so you have some time.

I don't hear anyone moving about above the stairs, and last I checked, they were all dining heavily on the wonderful things Glennis has produced from that kitchen of hers. Oh, how I miss being able to taste cream puffs and drink wine." He trailed off again, and this time I cleared my throat.

Friend or not, being able to run or not, I did need to move on if he had a way that he could help me.

"Very well." He clasped his hands in front of his waist. "Go to the river and find coins. Any coins that you can find. You will be able to use them to make calls that reach outside the inn. It does not matter who they belonged to. It only matters who you intend to call. I can't promise that this Love Ghost will answer your call, but it is the only way that I know we can contact someone from outside without inviting them in."

"Coins from the river?"

"Yes, coins from the river."

"Does it have to be water or the river specifically?" A thought had occurred to me about another mystery, and I wanted to test a theory.

"As far as I know, it does have to be from the river. You couldn't pilfer a coin from a fountain and be able to use it. The river has property in the flowing of water, and the life that has lived and died there that infuses the coins with abilities that a manufactured pond would not have."

"Fascinating."

"And useful. Now go corral your guests upstairs. It sounds like they are all moving out of the dining room, which means they could be about to bombard Hellen, which will make her unhappy. You should hear the way she swears upstairs sometimes when she thinks no one is listening. This particular crowd has given her more fits than even your eccentric writers' group was able to do. It seems they were into some trouble almost every day, and each one of them brought something ludicrous to her attention."

"She never said anything to me." Why hadn't she said anything to me?

"And why would she? You run the place like a well-oiled machine, and part of that is people who you delegate tasks to having the ability to actually handle those tasks. If they need you, they let you know, but they handle many things without having to bring it to your attention. You should be proud of them for that." He chuckled. "Plus, I know Hellen and Poobah have discussed that perhaps if they give you more room to not be involved in all the things of the inn, that perhaps you will convince your Dean to offer for your hand."

My perfect eyebrows crinkled again. "There are issues with that."

"But are there? Surely there is a way around the rules. Or perhaps with Amelia, there is a way to introduce them into your world?"

"That's a whole other set of issues."

"You might be surprised." He nodded as if coming to a decision. "You will need to go to the river and find coins. I feel in my soul, which you can see floating before you, that this is the way we will find this ghost you are questing for. You may bring the Love Ghost here when found, and we can talk with this entity together. I'd rather you not do it alone, if you don't mind."

I laughed derisively. "Yeah, no, I don't mind that at all. Should I be looking for any particular kind of coin, or is it anything goes?"

"Anything goes. Bring them to the phone booth tonight at midnight, and we'll see what we can find out."

"Thank you, Earl. I really appreciate this. I'm at a loss, and your help is invaluable."

Now it was his turn to laugh. "We'll see if I help at all. Hold your praise until we figure things out, young lady." With that, he vanished through the wall. It made me wonder why he was trying to open a door down here when he should have just been able to float through it. But since he was gone, and we had far more important things to do, I would have to hold my question for a later date.

Okay, so I needed to go down to the riverbank and see if I could find any coins. Easy peasy, right? Probably not, but it was necessary, so I went to my room and got my waders, then let Aunt Hellen know that I was going down to see Dean at the waterfront.

"Are you planning on walking across the Susquehanna in some sort of ritual?" She glanced down at the boots, then back up at my face.

I wasn't going to lie to her. "I am on a mission for coins."

"Don't we make enough money here that you don't have to scrounge around in the river, Roxy?"

"Yes, Aunt Hellen. I'll explain it later."

"I wait with breathless anticipation for that discussion, dear."

I was sure she would, but I didn't stay to banter with her when I had somewhere to be. On my trek down the hill to the river, I rehearsed what I'd say if Dean saw me. I couldn't exactly explain that a ghost in the house had told me to come find some old, dirty, and wet money so that I could call a Love Ghost. Somehow, that would be even worse than him finding the book about seducing your lover into a commitment.

But then, when I got to the river, I found Amelia also in waders and already in the shallows close to the bank. She was alone, which made me nervous until I glanced to the left and found Dean watching over her from the deck of the ferry as they waited for it to make its next launch.

I waved to him and then joined the young girl in the water. I didn't need an excuse this time, and if asked, I'd simply say I had seen her down here and wanted to find out what she was doing by joining her.

"Hey there, what are you looking for?"

She had the hem of her t-shirt billowed out like a basket, and I flinched at the silt that was staining the light pink material. Her laundry was not my problem, so I let it go.

"Oh, hi, Roxy! Uncle Dean is letting me wander around down here until we can go across the river. He's taking me to the camp to see about planning a surprise for my dad for his birthday. Don't tell him." Her eyes lit up, and her smile was contagious.

"I would never."

"I know, but I still have to say it, just in case."

"Understood." I eyed the t-shirt again and found that the whole thing was weighted down with tiny, shiny, round objects. "Are those coins?" I asked the question as nonchalantly as possible, but I could feel my excitement ramping up.

"Yeah. I figured that it can't be good for all this metal to be in the water, and some of them are really old. My dad said that there's a possibility that there might be something valuable in here. Even if there isn't, I figured maybe I could help pay for the surprise, and do some clean up at the same time." She pointed at the big plastic trash bag on the shore. "I'm also pulling out any trash that's gotten stuck in the piles of branches."

"That's wonderful. I'm so proud of you, and the city will be, too." This kid was something, always thinking beyond herself. I knew there was a part of me that wanted her to have the talent because it would bring her into the fold and possibly make things easier for me to have a full relationship with Dean. But I also thought that even if she didn't have an amazingly handsome and wonderful uncle, I would still want someone like her in our camp, simply because she, herself, was a wonderful person.

"Can I help?" I asked, pausing at the water's edge.

She closed her eyes, and little eddies started forming around her, tiny swirling patterns of water that looked like hiccups in the slowly moving current. I wondered if she knew she could do that, or if she didn't even realize she was doing it. So many questions I wasn't ready to face just yet.

When her eyes popped back open, she smiled and nodded. "Do you want to see my haul?"

"Always."

She very proudly showed me every piece of what she had in that t-shirt bowl, from the coins to the pieces of a belt buckle, to what looked like a brooch backing, a ring, and the standoff of someone's cell phone. Was there a cell phone also in the water somewhere?

But that question was whisked out of my head when she pulled the top of the t-shirt against her belly. "I want to see if any of these coins work in the phone booth again, as soon as you'll let me. I know you asked me to wait, and I promise I'll do that, but I also really think it will be cool to get back to it as soon as you're ready."

I hesitated, not sure what I wanted to say to her or how I wanted to say it. In the end, I nodded. "I'll let you know."

"I know you will. I trust you to tell me anything I need to know, and I know that you're always honest with me, so I will wait for as long as you say I should."

The guilt hit me like a ton of bricks right in the center of my chest. She trusted me to an extent I had not considered. We weren't going to be able to put this conversation off until a later date. I wasn't going to be able to keep pushing off when to talk to Caper. No matter what was going on around here, and no matter if Caper and Dean chose to move Amelia away from us,

I had to figure out how to ask if they were aware of Amelia's talent. Then I'd have to let the chips fall where they may.

It could break my heart, but I couldn't keep lying to people whom I loved so much, all four of them.

"I'll tell you what, why don't you get cleaned up and bring your dad with you? We'll see if one of your coins will work on the phone. I'd like to talk to whoever you were talking to."

"Do you think my dad will be angry that I've been sneaking up to the house, even though he thought I was in bed?"

That at least I could chuckle at and not lie at all. "He knows. He brought it up, and I told him that you were fine up there, and I didn't mind at all."

"Okay, phew." She smiled and started walking out of the river. I hadn't picked up anything like a coin from the silt or water, but maybe I didn't have to if we used one of hers.

"How about we meet up at the house in about an hour? I'll see if Poobah can be with us to make sure everything is right. He owned this place for a long time, so maybe he knows something we don't know."

"Sure thing. See you soon!"

I had some fast talking to do, though, with my family before I met Dean's family at the house. And I had to make sure that the other family was involved in something, either in a locked room in the house, or out of the house, before I opened that door under the stairs.

I only hoped no part of this was about to bite me hard in the rear end.

Famous last words...

Chapter 16

I t was not easy getting everyone I needed in the same place, while also keeping a different herd of people in another place that was anywhere, but where all those people were. Like I said, it's complicated, but I did it.

Shutting every guest and the help into the kitchen and dining room for appetizers and dinner allowed me to gather my family into the billiards room.

Yeah, we were back in the billiards room. I did not miss the way Poobah glanced down at the green fabric stretched across the pool table, taking a ball out of the left corner pocket and rolling it back and forth, but not looking at me.

"I have things to say, and I need you all to be quiet while I say them. There will be time for questions, and possibly some answers, if we have them after."

I waited a beat to see if Mena, Poobah, Aunt Hellen, or Uncle Vince would say anything to contradict me, but nothing came out of their mouths. I nodded and continued.

"There is something going on in this establishment, and in the cottage at the back of the property, that I don't know if we can ignore or put off anymore. Amelia has talent. I saw it today in the river when she was looking for coins and trash in the shallows. I asked if I could join her in helping, and when she closed her eyes, the water started swirling around her, as if to protect her in case I didn't wait for her acceptance of my help. She's been able to change the cloud formation and also sees a glow whenever Mena and I are connected with our magic. I know Dean can hear a hum when the books sparkle, but I don't believe Caper is in tune at all with this part of the world. That leads me to believe that the talent comes from Amelia's mother."

I folded my hands on the pool table and looked at each person in the room. They all meant the world to me, even if they sometimes tested the limits of my patience. We were a family, a weird one, but still a family.

"I also know that she can talk with people on the phone under the stairs. The line does not go out of this building, and I spoke with Earl to see if he was the one on the other end of the line, and he was not. He asked me to go to the river to get coins to make calls with spirits other than him. I didn't know that was possible."

No one said anything. I looked around the room, waiting for someone to chime in with a theory or an answer, but no one said anything.

"Well? Doesn't anyone have anything to add to that?" I leaned forward on my hands.

"You wanted us to wait until you were done," Poobah said, his brow furrowed, and his face drawn into a frown. "Are you done then?"

I rocked back on my heels and resettled my brain. These people were not the enemy. They were my family. I needed to treat them like we were all on the same team, because we were. "Yes, I'm done. Sorry."

"That's not how the thing is supposed to work," Aunt Hellen burst out. "It doesn't need coins at all. What does he mean by getting them from the river?"

"I have no idea, but Amelia was afraid she'd done something she wasn't supposed to because she'd talked to a man on the phone under the stairs, and then Earl said he hadn't talked to her, so I don't know who she would have talked to."

"You've been letting her into the phone booth?" Poobah asked in a deceptively calm voice, but I felt the undercurrents in each word.

"Yes, she has, PooBear, and there is nothing wrong with that," Mena said. "Why wouldn't we let her explore here, in a safe place, with safe people?"

"Because it sounds like it's not as safe as you'd like it to be, Philomena, and no matter how much you and your sister want to be able to pull Dean and his family into our world, this is not the responsible way to do it." Poobah cracked the ball in his hand onto the table, and I felt the vibration all the way through to my toes.

That didn't just rock me back on my heels—that punctured my lungs and my heart at the same time.

Uncle Vince was quick to place a hand under my elbow. "You're wrong, Poobah. For once, you're not only wrong, but also deflecting your error to someone else when you shouldn't be. I don't know what's gotten into you, but this has to stop. What are you even talking about?"

Poobah turned towards the door, and I really thought that he was going to leave. Things would never be the same if he chose to exit this conversation without answering. He had to know that.

And apparently he did, because he stopped himself from reaching for the doorknob. "There's far more going on than any of you realize," he said.

"Then tell us," I begged. "Just tell us what is going on in that head of yours, or even just what's going on with Glennis, or what's going on with your attitude change about Amelia and her family. You said before that the rules didn't always have to be followed, and yet here you are slamming us for doing exactly what you said was okay. What harm is there in letting Amelia use the phone booth? Tell us."

"The answer to that will take much too long to go into." He sighed and ran a hand through his gray hair. "Are you keeping her out of the phone booth until we figure out who exactly she talked to?"

"Yes," I said stiffly. "Of course, I am. You might not think I know what I'm doing, but I actually do."

"It's not that." He sighed again, and while normally I would feel sorry for him and bad that he was obviously stressed out, I couldn't find it in me to care at the moment.

"Then what is it? I need answers to many things, but this one feels like it's far more important than anything else going on right now, even finding a killer and trying to prove that Glennis didn't do it, even though I'm starting to have my doubts."

That got him to zero in on me. Good, let's go.

"Glennis would never kill someone, especially over a recipe card."

"Do you know that for certain?" I asked with some edge to my voice. I didn't like it, but I was tired of culling myself to please him. "Because when I mentioned it around town, there was a decided pause and even some gasping about the card and the wedding that never happened."

"What wedding?" Mena asked.

Poobah gave a sharp shake with his head, but I was way past listening at this point.

"Glennis was supposed to get married at the Justice of the Peace. She had everything set up, and then it was off, and she went full hermit, in the cottage out back, taking a job here in the kitchen and never leaving." How much should I go into? This was family, and even if Poobah didn't want to talk, then the rest of them had a right to know. "I found a book in the cottage that gave me quite the show when I asked it about helping me figure out the murder and what Glennis had to do with it. It told me to find the Ghost of Love and ask my questions. When I talked to Earl, he told me he had to look into some things, but that I'd have to get coins from the river to use for calls, and that's where I found Amelia, who was able to make currents in the water just by closing her eyes. You don't see how that's all related? What if she does something that she doesn't understand? What if she already has?"

Poobah closed his eyes and ducked his head to the point where his chin almost hit his bony chest. "I'll go talk to Glennis. It's time."

"And what exactly are you going to talk to her about?" Aunt Hellen asked for all of us.

"I will tell you after I tell her. I promise."

With that, he left, and we pretty much stared at each other without any words.

Finally, I found something to get the conversation rolling. "We have to talk with Caper and his family. I have research to do, and I asked Amelia to bring her family around in about thirty minutes. I can put her off for a little bit more, but I need help with this."

A series of nods followed, and I felt better for the first time in a little while. After handing out assignments for each of the people in the room, I left and headed right for my rooms. I had things to gather and a presentation to come up with on why it would be best for us to be able to teach the young Amelia that she had magic and how to use it. No pressure, no pressure at all.

Mena shoved my door open just as I was gathering my notes, scaring both me and my errant cat, Moose, who had decided to perch on the back of the sofa and watch me while I worked.

"What in the world is going on around here?" she asked, plopping onto the couch and immediately stroking my cat's back. Moose, for his part, purred so loudly that you could probably hear it out in the hallway. Then again, maybe you could hear it out in the hallway because Mena had not closed the door behind her.

I fixed that and then sat down next to her with my upturned hands in my lap and my ankles crossed.

"I talked with Chessie today."

"I did notice your lovely eyebrows. Good choice. I've been having this feeling that something monumental is about to happen, and you're going to want to look fabulous for it. Just saying."

"Like I need more pressure right now. Thanks?"

"We all have pressure, Roxy, and no matter what you think, or what Poobah tells you, I absolutely know that you are the best at handling all the things. It's why he agreed so readily to let you have the inn. He would have stayed on, straight through to his death, as the owner if I had been the one to ask."

"You really think so?" I had never even considered that. I'd thought he was ready to go, more than ready to start traveling and being able to let go of the responsibilities he had on the daily with running an inn. Had he left early to give me the space to call my own and make my own?

"Oh, my word, absolutely! Mom and Dad talked all the time about how he was never going to leave this place and that they'd find him some day, leaning over the ledgers, writing that one last entry before finally giving up the ghost."

"Seriously?"

"Seriously, Roxy. I don't think you always understand how much people trust you to do the right things and to do it well. You underestimate yourself, even while everyone else thinks you are absolutely amazing." She pulled Moose down onto her lap, and surprisingly, the cat stayed, still purring as he had before. "You don't have to use manipulation to get people to do what you want them to do. You trust that someone will do what you've asked of them and don't butt in unless it's absolutely necessary. That's a beautiful thing. By the way, Aunt Hellen wanted me to let you know that the cleaning ladies will handle the dust after the guests leave. Apparently, every time they've been in there to clean, there's someone sitting in the room, so they were trying not to be intrusive. See, you delegate, and you get answers. Even if I get told to give them by another delegator. Auntie Hell, in this instance."

My whole face felt like it was flaming red, so I kept my head turned away from Mena. "You're giving me far too much credit."

"No, I'm not. End of that discussion. On to what to do about the family down in the cottage."

The subject change was incredibly welcomed. While I wanted to immediately talk to the family, I also wanted to do this the right way.

"Before you start overthinking, let's get a few things straight," Poobah said from the doorway to my sitting room. I hadn't heard him open the door, and to be honest, I wished that he hadn't.

At least he closed it behind himself. He didn't come farther into the room. Instead, he hung back at the door with his hands behind him and his eyes closed.

I was not going to start this conversation because I didn't know which one we were having, and I didn't want to dig down into the wrong one.

"Silence is not always golden," he said once he opened his eyes.

Mena snaked her hand under Moose and touched the outside of my thigh. Sisterly boost achieved.

"I agree, but it appears that I'm not the one who chooses to remain silent," I said. "Why are you here?"

"Because I don't like where this is going, and it's not going to get better by hiding ourselves away."

"I'm not hiding anything from you. If it happens, you're aware of it. If you ask me a question, I will answer it to the best of my ability. What more do you want?"

Mena flicked me, which caused Moose to jump to the floor. He sauntered over to Poobah and then sat like a guardian between us and our grandfather.

"Honestly? I want this whole thing to stop. I don't have all the answers, and I'm sorry for coming off brutally in the billiards room." He ran a hand down over his face, pulling his chin and then shaking his head. "It was never supposed to be like this."

"Like what, Poobah? All I'm seeing is that there are secrets here that I'm in the dark about. Normally, I don't care because I don't need to know everything about everyone. I let my employees and my family do whatever is right for them with no judgment, the best I can. But this is different. If there's something I need to know about Glennis and how it pertains to the murder of a guest, then I'd ask you to spill it."

"Anthony Fromm. You want to know about him."

It almost sounded like an accusation, but I wasn't biting.

"I only have limited information from all those years ago." He brushed his hand over his hair again, what little of it was left. If he kept messing with it, he'd be bald.

"And I only want what would help me figure out who would kill Penny. I don't need to know all the ins and outs of everything, but if you want me to find a killer, and you're keeping info back from me, then there's no way you can expect me to succeed."

"Can I come in?" he asked, his voice weary, and his shoulders had drooped.

"Of course." Neither Mena nor I moved. There was a wing-backed chair across from us. He used to sit there when I'd first taken over ownership of the inn. We'd pore over the ledgers and the supplies. He'd help me make plans for the upcoming week and only jump in when he truly thought I wasn't getting something. Mostly, he'd let me make mistakes in a safe place, ones that didn't hurt anyone, but me and my brain.

Taking up the seat, he leaned his head back for a moment and then leaned forward with his elbows on his knees and his hands clasped in front of him. "Long, long ago."

"In a galaxy far, far away?" Mena asked jokingly.

He smiled, and that at least broke the tension for just a minute. "Look, I don't want to tell this story, and I need you to keep it to yourself. I don't want Glennis to know all the details. I made that decision thirty years ago, and I can't unmake it now. I need your promise that what is said in this room stays in this room. Agreed?"

"Absolutely," Mena chimed in almost immediately.

I hesitated, though. What if it was something that shouldn't be kept to myself? What if something horrible had happened, and I wouldn't be able to ever look Glennis in the eyes again once I knew her secrets?

"Roxanne?" he said.

Almost no one ever called me that, so I knew this was serious. And I could handle anything that was thrown my way. I'd proven that time after time, and it was no less true right now.

"Agreed."

He blew out a breath and closed his eyes again. Leaning back in the chair, he gripped the armrests like I had when I was about to have Chessie rip the hair right out of my face.

How bad could this be?

Chapter 17

"Thirty years ago, Glennis was in love with Anthony Fromm. He came from a prominent family in the area, and he was a nice guy. I liked him a lot when I saw him around town. He was a little older than she was, but they had a lot in common, and they quite obviously loved each other." He popped his eyes open. "This was a match made in whatever heaven you believe in. Glennis was collecting kitchen supplies and scoping out apartments in the area. They weren't going to use his family's money for anything. Anthony had been trying to break away for at least five years, and he was ready to do that with Glennis."

"What did his family do?" Mena asked.

"They had a mill that they ran for many years in a town about thirty miles from here, until it shut down and was moved elsewhere. But they still had the money and the connections, a lot of money and a lot of connections. Anthony was the next in line when he came here for college, and he wanted no part of that legacy. He'd told his father about meeting Glennis, and his father allowed him to date her, but always reminded Anthony it couldn't last forever."

"Why not? Because she wasn't the stock?" I asked derisively.

"No, because he had already been promised to someone years ago, and she was waiting back at home for him to return and marry her."

"Betrothal?" Mena asked, as Moose jumped back into her lap. She ran her hand over his back, and the engine rumble of his purr started back up.

"Of a sort. It wasn't anything set in stone. Heck, it wasn't even written as a contract. But his family was completely against anything more than leading Glennis along and letting Anthony sow his wild oats before settling down on the path that had been laid out for him since he was five."

"Five? How do you know who your child will marry at five?"

"It's similar to the arrangement that your ultimate grandmother was bound to, so I understood when he told me that he and Glennis were just going to get married at the courthouse, and his family could disown him if they wanted to. I'd already set Glennis up as the head cook and was willing to let them stay in the cottage while they figured things out, but Anthony didn't want to be beholden to anyone."

"How would that have made them beholden to you?" It was a serious question because I worried that Caper would feel the same way if I sprang this magic thing on him and he had to choose between going along with me to keep the house he'd recently made into the first safe home his children had. I didn't want that.

"They weren't." Poobah picked at the covers on the armrest. "They wouldn't have been, but I couldn't convince Anthony of that, and Glennis would have followed him anywhere. In fact, she did follow him a lot of places, unsure if he would be able to actually stand up to his family in the end, or if he'd leave her at the cheap justice altar because he was going back without her."

The hair on the back of my neck stood up as my mind raced along how this whole story could end. There were few good endings, considering that Glennis was still single thirty years later and held onto the recipe card that was supposed to have been her first married-woman offering to celebrate the marriage.

"So, when she saw him get on the ferry to cross the river, she figured he was leaving her. He never took the ferry unless he had to visit his family, and he'd told her he'd cut off all communication."

"So, he just left, and she came back haunted by the loss?" Mena asked.

"No, he died in a boating accident, according to Chessie," I said, pulling the info to the forefront of my brain.

"That was the story," Poobah said.

"Hold on, what do you mean that was the story?" I reached out a hand to pet Moose to ground myself, and he let me.

"Well, it wasn't boating as he was actually on the ferry. He'd driven his car up the ramp and sat in the vehicle halfway across the river. Glennis had seen him and tried to get on board at the last minute. She was sure she could convince him not to go. I told her it might be better coming from me. She trusted me, so she agreed to let me go after him instead. I waited for him to get out of his car. When he finally did, I confronted him about the decision he was making. He said something particularly nasty, and I decked him in the mouth. He fell over the side of the ferry, got caught on something that dragged him under the boat, and drowned."

"Oh, no!" My hand went to my heart, and Mena gasped.

"Or at least that's what I told her." Poobah closed his eyes again, and I held my breath.

What did that mean?!?!

"Wait, what?" Mena asked for me. I nudged her with my shoulder in thanks.

"That's what I told her happened. She wouldn't have been allowed at the funeral anyway, and she had no contact with his family. There was no one within his parents' circle that she could reach out to. I told her what happened, but asked that she not tell anyone, or ask any questions, or I might get in trouble, since I had been the one who delivered the punch that probably sent him over the railing."

"So, you told her that you might have potentially killed him, and she believed you?" No way. "And that's what she has over you." It made sense on the surface, but not if you knew Poobah. "Why on earth did she believe you?"

"I can be very persuasive when I want to be. I might not have Mena's talents, but I'm not without talent at all."

"You charmed her and lied to her?" I grabbed a pillow to tuck against my stomach, then dug my fingers into Moose's fur. He must have known I needed the anchor because he didn't move.

"I did. He wasn't coming back. I did punch him, but he didn't fall over the railing, and he certainly didn't drown. I watched him drive off the ferry, tears running down his face from the decision he had made. There was no way he was going to be able to marry Glennis, and he couldn't face marrying the woman he'd been promised to. He knew things about his family's business, and he was being pressured to turn state's evidence against his family. In order to give those details that the government was looking for, he had to disappear."

"Glennis would have gone with him," Mena said in a small voice.

"She probably would have, but that was not offered. In fact, it was turned down when he asked. It was all or nothing, and if he did nothing, then he was going to get roped into the conspiracies and the investigation. He would have had to pay for crimes he had not done."

"Wow." Mena and I said the word in stereo, then looked at each other before looking back at Poobah.

"I can't tell her I lied to her all those years ago. It would do nothing but hurt her, and I already did enough of that. I have given her freedom and passes, as you call them, on a pretty permanent basis because I should never have stepped in, but I can't step out. If I had known she would carry that forward to you, I might have made a different choice, but I can't undo things now. I did the best that I could when I was in the middle of a bad situation. I couldn't see that far ahead to know how it would play out."

"She didn't defy you and talk with his family?" I had to know because the Glennis I had interacted with for all these years would not have let one person tell her what she could or could not do.

"It's hard to explain how broken she was. She operated like a robot for weeks after he was gone. I kept waiting for her to cry or rail at the world, but it never happened. She just seemed to shut down. And when she opened back up, she did not want to talk about it. She would cut me off any time I tried to talk to her, and eventually, I stopped trying."

"What is the significance of the recipe card?" It had just popped into my head.

"He gave it to her right before he left. In her mind, it was the last thing he touched before he died."

"Damn." There was that word again.

"Yes."

We all sat for a minute or two in complete silence, except for Moose, who started back up with his purring.

"But why did Penny have the recipe?" I asked.

"That I can't answer." Poobah rose from his spot on the chair and leaned over to kiss both me and Mena on our foreheads. "I will say that I stand behind my statement about not letting Amelia play in the phone booth. I didn't state my thoughts in the right way. I should have stopped and thought about how to say it before I opened my mouth, but I had so much going on in my head with this Glennis situation and the murder. I'm not against us talking with Caper, and even Dean, about the possibility of Amelia having powers. But we have to have it be a focused conversation, and it has to be well-thought-out. I know that you want this, and I want it for you, too. I love you, and I love him, but we have to make sure we do this in a responsible way and not in the middle of a murder investigation. That might be too much on your plate all at the same time."

"I already told them to come by in ten minutes. I can just tell them it's about wanting Isaac to look deeper into Penny's past and maybe Anthony's." My balloon was deflated about getting this taken care of right now, but I completely agreed with him. It had waited this long. It could wait a little longer until we found the murderer.

Poobah lifted my face by placing his hand under my chin. "I was hoping you might say that. I know it's difficult, believe me, I do, but I hope this will be the right way to do it so that you get what you want, but also protect a very young girl who might have no idea what she's capable of. Her whole family will possibly struggle with this. We're going to need time and space for them to do that, and we don't have it with a murder hanging over our heads."

My eyes filled with tears, but I nodded.

He walked out of my sitting room, pulling the door closed gently behind him. Mena didn't say anything for a few minutes, then she scooped Moose up and placed him on the back of the couch. After a big stretch, he settled in. Mena smiled, then sank to her knees in front of me. Clasping my hands in hers, she leaned forward until our foreheads touched.

"You are the strongest person I know, and you're also the smartest. Let's solve this damn thing so we can move forward. I want the vacation, I want your staycation for you, I want us to go back to no murders." She leaned back so that we were facing each other at a better distance to look into each other's eyes. "We're going to get it all, but first we have to get every piece of information to solve this thing. So, what do we need first? I can go talk to Micah whenever you need me to."

I saw the slight tinge to her cheekbones when she said Micah's name. Maybe she'd be coming back to stay after all. "You know if you end up with him, I'm going to demand that you get monogrammed towels that say M&M. I'll pay for them myself."

She giggled, but she didn't deny the possibility. Good enough.

I ran down the things we knew about Penny, often stepping away at family outings, and the info Caper gave me about her being in the gazebo until she got a signal, either from her phone or the light in the third-story window, that sent her scurrying. After that, I told her about the Ghost of Love. The teddy bear she already knew about, and shot off a quick text to Micah to see if he'd be willing to share any info about any movement they saw in the room. He didn't get back to her right away, but most likely he was working the case and would respond as soon as he had a moment.

We were down to about one minute until we would be invaded by the Winchester/Manchester clan. I wanted them in the library this time, where I could see if any sparkles came out of books with Amelia in the room. Plus, we'd be far away from the family of guests, and I needed that.

Just so that we weren't overwhelming anyone, I asked Mena to join me in the library and requested that Poobah, Uncle Vince, and Aunt Hellen take up posts to keep the other family out of here.

There were a number of sitting areas in the two-story library, and all of them were comfortable. I spotted Isaac carrying a laptop with him, through the window, and quickly changed our sitting area to be around a table. I would have preferred the beautifully upholstered chairs, but that would have made Isaac keep the computer on his lap, where we wouldn't be able to see what he'd found.

Amelia was in the door first, skipping along the carpet, with a small bag that clinked with her every move. Right, the pay phone. I had said we'd try it out with her coins, and I promised to have Poobah there. Okay. I'd pivot to that, just as soon as I could get Isaac to tell me what he knew and share a little of what I knew to put him on the path I needed him on.

Isaac followed close behind. His gaze kept darting everywhere all at once. I was afraid he was going to send himself into a panic until his dad put a hand on his shoulder, and he immediately went still. A smile popped out on the young man's face, and he completed the rest of his journey in a leisurely stroll.

Caper was next. He trailed his hand over the woodwork of the shelves and seemed to walk his fingers over the book spines of our rare first editions. Well, at least the ones I let stay out in the open part of the library. The others were in the glass case with the big book of Scottish myths.

I waved them over to the table, then smiled when Isaac immediately took up a spot and opened his laptop. He hit some keys, and a screen popped up that looked like a wild salad of words. Hopefully, he'd have the patience to explain what he'd done to those of us who didn't work with that kind of chaos.

Caper put a hand on Issac's shoulder again as he started bouncing in his chair. He settled down just like he had last time. Was I watching a father with a son he knew well enough that they didn't need words, or was Caper the one with the magic? There was no way he and Dean were related to me, or they would have been informed of the possibility of magic long, long ago, so I wasn't worried about us being on the same family tree. And yet, if they were the ones with the magic and also didn't know it, then the concept might be easier for them to comprehend.

I put that aside since that was not the subject we were pursuing. No, we were going to put some ideas together and get several steps closer to the killer's identity. I could feel it in the energy of the library.

"Thanks for coming over, everyone," I said after everyone had taken a seat at the table.

"I was told in no uncertain terms that I was either to be here or I would never be spoken to again." Caper leaned over and patted Amelia's hands. She'd put the bag of clinking coins at her elbow and was staring intently at me. I hoped I wasn't going to disappoint her.

"Well, however you managed to be coerced into being here, we're happy." Mena had taken the spot right next to me. Dean, Caper, Isaac, and Amelia had chosen seats on the opposite side of the table. I didn't want it to feel like we were at a negotiations table, but there was nothing I could do about it now without making things awkward.

"Okay, so I invited you here to talk about a few things. Isaac, do you want to go first? I can see you're pretty much chomping at the bit to show us what you've found."

Amelia groaned at my words, but one look from her father had her quieting down.

"I promise you're next, Amelia." I smiled at her, and she ducked her head with a shy smile of her own.

"So, I made a slideshow to be able to keep things in order."

A slideshow? Holy cow.

"Do you need a projector?" I asked.

"Do you seriously have one in here? Because that would be so awesome."

I did, and his enthusiasm made me giggle as I rose from my chair. It was anchored on a shelf and hidden as a long, decorated wood panel. I popped the latch and snagged the cord that fell out. I dragged the screen down and anchored it to the floor. I peeked behind me, and there was Dean watching me with a little smile on his full lips. Lovely.

I didn't take my time going back to standing at my full height. I flipped the lights off in our section as I walked past the wall and then turned my chair around at the table to be able to appreciate what Isaac had done with his slideshow. Mena joined me.

"We should have popcorn," she whispered, and I giggled again. I felt the tension leave my body, at least until we got to what Isaac had found, and if it put someone else in the spotlight or at least proved that it wasn't Glennis.

"I can take questions along the way. I have notes that aren't on the slideshow itself. These are just my bullet points."

What a gem. I didn't get to spend much time with him because he was often in his room, doing his own thing. I would have to make more of an effort going forward. For the moment, I tuned back into what he was saying.

"So, we're going to start out with this Walter guy. I think you'll find it very interesting that when I called him to see about doing an apprenticeship, he was very happy to learn that I was studying his same profession as a private investigator."

Well, now, wasn't that fascinating?

Chapter 18

"Walter was a private investigator?" I asked, hoping I hadn't just cut Isaac off in his presentation, but my mind was whirling with all kinds of questions. He was lucky that was the only one I let loose when I had about forty-five others on the tip of my tongue.

"Yep, he's getting older and feels that since he has no children, no one to take over his firm, that having an apprentice might be exactly what he's looking for. Apparently, he just closed up a big case, as of yesterday, and so it would be the perfect time to go over some of the smaller ones he's done and those he still has to do. We have an interview on Friday if we discover he wasn't the one who killed Penny."

Gobsmacked. It was the only word I could think of to explain what I was feeling at this very moment. "But he said he was a painter, and had a show coming up at a gallery, so he needed the room to finish out his collection."

"That was a lie." Isaac flipped to the next slide. "He has several personas that he'll use if he's on a case. The art thing is just one of them, but he finds that it can get him a pass to be broody and not talk to anyone he doesn't want to because he can pretend he has so many things happening in his creative brain that he can't stop for idle chitchat."

"I looked him up online." I felt lied to because I had been lied to.

"He has a few websites set up under each of his names. For the last ten years, he always goes by Walter because one time he forgot to answer when someone called out the name he'd given them when they met. He almost botched the whole thing, so now he goes by Walter, but with different last names depending on the background he's going with."

The next slide was a teddy bear that looked very familiar. The ears were the same, the paws were the same. It even had a ribbon tied around its neck just like the one found in Penny's room, but this ribbon was blue instead of yellow.

"Now, sometimes he uses cameras set up in these stuffed animals to capture anything that happens in a room. His recent client had asked for one, and he's trying to figure out how to get it back since someone took it as part of an investigation." He looked particularly pleased with that piece of information, and I couldn't say that I blamed him.

"Are you telling him that you know Penny?" I asked.

"Nope, he just likes to talk. I've heard that from several PIs, since they can't usually talk about their work and they're not out partying without a job to do while they're on the dance floor. He doesn't want to have someone spot him and not be able to explain why he's at one place after being somewhere completely different before."

"And you want that for your life?" Caper took his measure from his post next to his son.

"Nah. Part of apprenticing, as you know from your own career-building skills, doesn't mean you have to make the same decisions as your mentor. It means you can learn from them and make different choices based on a good foundation."

"Are you sixteen or forty, Isaac?" Mena grinned, and he grinned back at her.

"Moving on." He flipped to the next slide. "I've done some pre-emptive research on every member of the family that's here. I didn't find much, though Leon is a tad bit shady for a professor. I didn't want to completely deep dive because I thought it might be a waste of time, and I do still have homework to do."

Caper laughed and elbowed him in the thigh. "That's not going to change anytime soon. You can do all this at the same time. It'll help with time management skills."

"Right, Dad. Thanks, Dad."

"Brat."

"Sure, Dad." He chuckled and moved on. "I'll look into Leon more because I think he has some things that don't add up." He moved to the next slide. "I also found out that this memoir, which Jessica thinks is dead and destroyed, is not necessarily a closed case. Some of those side trips Penny made appear to lead to the library."

The room went dark as he turned off his presentation.

No one had to be told to clap, and we all started at the exact same time.

He grinned again as I turned the lights on. "Sorry, I don't have more."

"Holy cow, Isaac, that's amazing. What you do have is phenomenal and so much more than I've been able to find out, wandering around town and getting my eyebrows waxed."

"They look beautiful, by the way," Dean said and blew me a kiss. Silly man, but that didn't mean I didn't blush.

"So, we have more people to look into. I can ask questions of the staff, and the family, and then the people themselves with this kind of background at my fingertips. Thank you, Isaac." I smiled at him, and he ducked his head.

"Just playing around."

"Hardly that." Shaking my head, I waited until he looked at me. "You're really good at this, and you should own it, not shy away from it."

Mena cleared her throat behind me. I ignored her.

"I..." he started, then trailed off.

"It's something to work on from what I've been told." That got Mena to laugh, so I moved on. "Let's divvy up some of this follow-up and see if we can't get the murderer in our crosshairs."

Everyone stared at me for further instructions, but I hadn't thought that far ahead yet.

I had brought my notebook of suspects and information along with me, so I took my time looking it over and then made some additional notes. Giving myself that pause allowed me to see how this could be accomplished in the best way. I guess I wasn't such a bad general, after all. Not that I'd tell Mena about the thought, or she'd crow it out to everyone who would listen.

"Here's what we've got. Isaac is going to do the deeper dive on Leon and keep up his conversation with Walter, just in case the man lets anything slip. He'll also be doing his homework, so we need to divide up the rest." I bit my lip while making a few more notes. "Mena, why don't you go after Micah for what's on that teddy bear cam footage. Dean, you said you have some feelers you'd put out, so maybe you and Caper can work on pulling in any info from there. I'll get Poobah, Uncle Vince, and Aunt Hellen to do some looking into the other family members so that I have more background to go after them with when it's time to question them. That will free up some of your time, Isaac, which should make your father happy." I glanced around the room and found everyone nodding at me. Excellent.

"And where does that leave you, dear sister?" Mena asked.

"Heading to the library. If anyone knows books, it's me. Maybe I can get some of the dirt from the librarian. If not, maybe I'll just ask the books to help me, and we'll go from there." Mena's eyes widened for a moment as if I'd taken her off guard, as everyone else laughed at what they thought was a joke. But I was very much not kidding.

And that not kidding followed me into the amazing library down the street from the inn. The Civil War had not made it this far north, so our library wasn't an old field hospital like one of the towns farther south, but the ferry had played an important role in transportation, and that counted in all our books.

The building was only open for another hour for me to do what needed to be done. I wasted no time walking myself down each aisle, both looking for someone to talk to who worked there and also keeping a very close eye out for any sparkles. The last set from the big book about the Love Ghost might not have come to fruition the way I thought they would, but that hadn't cut my desire to see the fireworks again and hopefully find something I could follow this time. I wanted the memoir, and if I could get my hands on it, then I would be a very happy inn owner and amateur sleuth.

Nothing popped out at me from the shelves, but I did end up running into Maribeth Johns in the mystery section. Perfect.

She'd been a librarian for as long as I'd been alive. Her enthusiasm for my enthusiasm for her favorite thing in the world had only grown my desire to devour every single book I could get my hands on. I didn't know why I wanted them all at once when I was very young, but she was all too happy to supply my every demand.

At one point, I had very much considered being a librarian, actually, thinking, what better place to have everything at your fingertips? But then I realized that it could have been incredibly disruptive if I were always surrounded by the tools of my trade. What if a time came when I wouldn't be able to stop myself from automatically reaching for a book and answering any questions, no matter how silly. With the number of people who populated this place and how often they came in, I thought hard about the possibility that someone would pick up on what I was doing and question why I always had to open a book to be able to answer the simplest of things if it was in my hand.

So, I had settled on being the next owner of the inn. I still had a library, though it wasn't as extensive as this one, but it was my own. It was better this way. Being surrounded by books all the time might sound like a dream come true, but it also could have been a distraction I didn't need.

As if to prove my point, almost every book on the third shelf to my left lit up with sparkles. What on earth was that?

Maribeth pulled my focus away from wondering which to pick up first by greeting me.

"Long time, no see! I always loved when you'd waltz in here and shout, 'Today is a good day to be at the library,' and then you'd squeal with glee and run to whatever section you wanted to look through that day, even the nonfiction devoted to antique cars."

"Those were the days," I said, giving her the softest smile, even as I was practically vibrating to reach out to every single book here.

"They were. And we have so many people bringing their kids in to look things up and to just be in this environment. I love it." She scoffed at herself. "But I'm sure that's not why you're here. What can I help you find?"

I hadn't exactly worked out how I wanted to broach the subject of the memoir. Isaac had said that it wasn't dead in the water, but I hadn't taken the time to ask what exactly he meant before I hustled myself down here. Dang!

"Hold on, before you say anything, I did want to mention that one of your guests was here almost every single day during what she kept saying was a family vacation that she had to get away from. A bit strange, but everyone has something." She folded her lips in and sighed. Then she grumbled. "What was her name! I can't believe I can't remember!"

"That's okay." My shoulders slumped. It really wasn't, since I had several women in the group and couldn't exactly ask each one if it was them, since Jessica had been very adamant about the memoir being a thing that should have never been born and most certainly dead. Dang again. Maybe one of the sparkly books would give me a better idea of who to go to, once I got Maribeth to leave me alone, and I could pretend like I was browsing as I was working my magic.

"Oh, I can't believe I can't remember her name. She doesn't have a library card here since she doesn't live around here, but that won't help you. Although I guess I'm making a mountain out of an ant hill. You probably don't care about where your guests are, as long as they're not getting into trouble."

Oh, I definitely wanted to know, but now I couldn't ask without seeming strangely interested when I obviously shouldn't be, according to Maribeth. At least, I couldn't without tipping my hand that I was looking into things. Although why couldn't I tell Maribeth just that? It wasn't like no one knew that I had looked into the previous two murders, and maybe if I told her, it would jog her memory.

"Wait!" she said before I could get a single word out. "She had on some very fancy shoes the one day. Actually, I think it was yesterday, or maybe it was today? We've had a bunch of programs with the kids, and all the days seem to run together."

"Were they pink?" I asked. Sylvie, again, possibly?

"Yes! Yes, they were! I was surprised that she'd want to walk around in those for everyday wear, but who am I to judge?"

"That's not judgment, just observation." Just like I was observing that every book on that shelf had suddenly gone dark. Had they all wanted to tell me that it was Sylvie? Or had I missed the opportunity to get more information because I hadn't been fast enough? I could still stick around and look through each of them to see if I could get any information, but I also wanted to get back to the inn as soon as possible. I had questions, and maybe, finally, I had someone to ask them to.

"Anyway, I'll leave you to your browsing. It's good to see you in here. I've missed you while you've been getting the inn up and running and looking into the last couple of murders. When I heard you were instrumental in solving them, I wasn't surprised, given all the mysteries you loved to read when you were younger. I tried to get you interested in the romances, but you just weren't having any of it. You wanted the puzzles, as your mom used to say."

The puzzles. So incredibly true. I had loved them, and that made sense as to why I kept getting involved in these things, outside of just wanting to irritate Norm and fearing that he was incapable of doing his job.

"I'll leave you to it then. You're in the right section, after all." She patted me on the hand and then left me there in the stacks.

Suddenly, a book lit up at my elbow. I grabbed it before the glow could fade. I had not read the author before, but I wasn't looking to be entertained at this point. I was looking for information. If this book helped, though, I might check it out and see what it was really about.

"I need help, right now. Point me in the right direction, please." I stuck my finger in the middle of the book, closed my eyes, and then flipped the book open. The shower of color wasn't as overwhelming as the book of myths, but I didn't need it to be.

Glennis is the point.

Well, I would have preferred that not be the message.

Chapter 19

My absolute need to run home, pull Glennis aside, and force answers out of her almost caused me to fly out of the library without even checking the book out. But as soon as I rounded the corner, I saw Maribeth standing at the counter. At the same moment, I realized I still had the book in my hand and couldn't exactly walk out the door without checking it out.

There was a short line at the counter, a few people in front of me who chatted it up with Maribeth, as you should when you were at the library. But I could feel my anxiety and desire to run creeping up with every second. I needed to calm the heck down. Two minutes was not going to change anything, but if I pushed my way forward, I would definitely set a very weird tone with the people in town that I hoped would recommend their relatives or out of town friends stay with me.

I told myself to calm down. I had time, and I had a cellphone. Grabbing it out of my purse, I sent a quick text to Mena, asking that she check in on Glennis and hold her in place until I returned.

Then I booked it back to the inn and hoped to be able to catch Sylvie, the pink shoe-wearer, before she clicked her way off to somewhere else.

The trek wasn't far, and I appreciated that. Being in a small town definitely had its benefits sometimes, especially when I rarely drove around if I could walk and make my exercise watch happy.

It pinged a chime of success as I mounted the stairs to the inn. I had things to do and places to be, but I was happy to know that I had achieved at least one goal today.

My first stop was the kitchen, just to check in with Glennis. She had no idea that we knew about her past, and I tried to keep that under wraps per Poobah's request as I opened the kitchen door to find her sitting at the table with Mena.

"What is it that you want? I can't seem to get rid of this girl, even after I gave her ice cream. I'm in no danger that I know of, since I had nothing to do with the murder, anyway, so I don't need someone to watch my every move."

I had my doubts about her totally being in the clear, but I kept those to myself, too.

"We have some new information, and I'm trying to nail down the details before I go search out other people I want to talk to. Thanks for staying put." I eyed the empty bowl that had traces of mint chocolate chip ice cream in it, sitting in front of Mena. "You're going to ruin your dinner."

"Not at all. I'm not leaving for another four hours." She looked up at the clock on the stove. "Micah's picking me up to go to the Wooden Nickle for a late dinner, so I needed something to tide me over. Glennis was nice enough to help me."

Glennis scoffed. "You helped yourself. And you need to be careful of that Micah boy. He does everything he can to sidetrack Norm so that he can take all the credit for any case that they can put to rest. I've seen it, if you don't believe me." She huffed out a breath and crossed her arms over her stomach.

I was not touching that with a ten-foot baguette. I shot Mena a look to let her know she wasn't either. She simply set her spoon into her bowl and pushed it back into the center of the prep table.

"How about you rinse that and put it in the dishwasher? I know you don't usually, but it's good to do something new every once in a while." Glennis chuckled as Mena shot me a nasty look.

Chuckling Glennis was exactly what I had been going for, so I'd take the verbal scolding from Mena later if she felt the need to dole it out.

"Now, Glennis, I have a question, and it might seem weird, but are you absolutely certain that you've never met Penny before? Maybe under a different name or many years ago, and so you just don't quite recall?"

She shook her head, then paused and looked up to the left. I had hope for a brief second, until she looked back at me again and shook her head once more. "No, I even tried talking to her once about what she'd like for the brunch since she'd only asked for that. I thought maybe I could talk her into at least letting me prepare a picnic or two while they were here. I didn't know if she knew that it could be done. But she cut me off after two words, telling me that she had no use for me, except for one thing, and that one thing I'd better do incredibly well. She was the one who asked for the recipe on the card."

"By name?"

She chewed on her lip for a few seconds. "No, not by name necessarily, but she told me there was a recipe that she'd heard about from a friend of hers, and it had to do with all the ingredients listed on the card. She said it had a weird name that sounded like fritter, and I asked if she meant the frittata. I've made it for many of our guests throughout the years, so I thought maybe it had been recommended by someone who had stayed here before. After agreeing that must be it, she walked away, but I caught her glance back at me with her mouth pursed and her eyes squinted. At that point, I vowed to myself that I would make the very best version of this thing that I'd ever made and show her that whatever her issue was, it shouldn't be with me."

"So, we didn't make the menu on that?"

"No, or if she had a different idea at the outset, she changed it with me." She shrugged her shoulders. "I was happy to make it. Some things had been coming up lately that were bringing me many memories, and making that frittata only seemed to soothe me, so I was happy to do it, even with her nasty attitude."

Should I ask? I was going to ask. "Why were the memories coming up? What memories?"

"I'd rather not talk about it. I told you that there are things I want to leave in the past, and that I can't say everything. Just let it be, Roxy."

I peered at her, willing her to understand that whatever she told me, I would take it in stride. Especially since I already knew the story from Poobah's side, but really wanted to hear it from her side. Sometimes my grandfather could be known to exaggerate if he thought it would make him look better. Did he really chase this Anthony away? Did he confront him? Or did he just talk to him briefly on shore, get his side of things, and decide for Glennis that she was better off without him?

I wouldn't put it past him, to be honest, but I had no idea how to convince her of that without tipping my hand on how much I knew. I wished I hadn't promised that I would act like I didn't know anything about her story.

But my hands were tied. I'd come up with something else to make the conversation happen. I just had to think about it some more.

"Well, stay safe. I know you don't think you're in danger, but there's a reason why that recipe seems to keep popping up. I just don't know what it is. But I will find out whether you tell me about the memories or not."

"I told you to let it be." She scowled at me to the point where she probably could have boiled water with her gaze alone.

"And I told you that I will prove that you aren't the murderer. And I'll do whatever I have to in order to make that happen. None of your secrets would ever turn me away from you. Nothing you could have done would make me love you less, Glennis. I don't need to know all the details, but if there is something that you're holding back that could crack this whole thing open, I wish you'd tell me so I could get this solved and get everyone out on their vacation."

I left it and her at that. Motioning Mena to follow me, I waited in silence while she rinsed out her ice cream bowl and then dutifully put it in the dishwasher. Glennis turned her back to us as she conveniently made sure that Mena had placed it correctly. I couldn't tell if she was seething or crying, and at this point, I was not in a place or a mindset to ask. She was safe, and we were on a mission.

As soon as we stepped out into the hallway, I turned to my sister. "We need what was on that footage from the room. Any luck with Micah the Magnificent?"

"Hey, at least he's not in my phone as Hottie like Dean has you."

"Don't even tell me that you wouldn't love it if that was the name that came up when you texted Micah."

She kept her mouth shut because she couldn't deny it and make me believe it.

"I know you have dinner with him tonight and that you probably planned on schmoozing him into sharing the info with you, but I don't think we can wait four or five hours. Is there any way you could get some kind of gift from Glennis for all his hard work and then deliver it to him before the dinner?"

"Well, you kind of shot that down when you just doubled down on her and tried to guilt her into telling you what you wanted to know. We really need to work on your skills, sister mine. There are ways with far more finesse than you appear to have."

Closing my eyes, I took a deep breath and then let it out. "That's a chore for another day. Right now, I need less finesse and more action. I have to find Sylvie and see if I can get her to tell me why she was at the library every day and what she was looking for. And then I need to see if I can get her to share the memoir with me. I also have questions about what she was doing in Leon and Sally's room and why she hid under the bed when Sally banged on the door to be let in."

"You have a lot to do. I'll leave you to it and see if I can smooth things over with Glennis with a little finesse. You might not like it, or think it takes too long, but you don't have my level of experience." She fluffed her hair like she was preparing for an audition or a role, then plastered a tiny frown on her face and opened the door back up into the kitchen. At the last second, she turned around and blew me a kiss, then began her tour de force.

"Glennis, I know Roxy can be abrupt and a meany, and I'm so sorry about that. I tell her often that she needs to really take some of those continuing education classes on people skills, but do you think she ever listens to me?"

The door closed behind her on Glennis's laugh. I rolled my eyes and went to do the things I was good at.

Sylvie's room was down the hallway from the top of the stairs. She was three rooms away from Sally and Leon and on the opposite side of the hallway. I had no idea if she was actually in there, but it made sense to at least start here instead of going into every nook and cranny around the inn, only to find out she was resting on her bed.

I knocked several times and called out to her. I was never sure if people had headphones on or earbuds in, and I hated to leave without being absolutely certain that the person I was looking for was not actually in their room. I heard something hit the floor with a thud, like I had when she'd ducked under the bed in Leon's room, and wondered if that was a thing with her.

"Sylvie, I just have a quick question about something I found in the library that I thought you might be interested in, if you don't mind opening the door. It will only take a moment. I promise." Lying was not always my strong suit, but it was easier when the person I was trying to convince wasn't looking right at me.

Finally, the door cracked open, and Sylvie stuck her head out with a smile. What was she hiding in there?

I might never know if she didn't open the door wider, but I couldn't exactly force it. I did have some lines I didn't cross, after all.

"Hi there," I said, as if it wasn't strange that she was hiding her whole body behind a door. "Do you have a minute to come down to the library? I found something that you might want to look at. I ran into the librarian today, and she said you were really into researching, showing up every day, and looking through books. I have a whole section that might interest you."

"Can we do it a different time? I'm in the middle of something."

"Got it. I am, too. Trying to figure out who killed Penny has taken up a lot of space in my head, and that's why I forgot to ask you about writing the memoir for her. Do you know what your mother-in-law, Jessica, meant when she said that there was one reason that it should have never been written?" I was gambling a lot here, but I also had a very distinct feeling in my gut that if I didn't press now, I might never get the chance again.

"You know what, I think I can swing the time right now. The rest can wait. I wasn't the one who wrote the memoir, though. I was just filling in research for Penny. My mother-in-law will be incredibly angry if she finds out I helped, so I'd really appreciate it if you'd keep it to yourself."

"Of course." That was easier than I thought it would be, and it made me nervous. But I was in now and couldn't back out.

Sylvie very carefully slipped out of the door and then yanked it closed behind her. Unlike last time, I didn't catch a glimpse of anything that would have set off my radar, but I didn't even know what that could have been if I did see it.

I waved Sylvie in front of me, and she stalked off down the hall. I noticed that she was wearing sneakers instead of her pink heels.

Which is the only reason I can think of that I fell, literally, for her next move.

As we reached the landing, I glanced up to see that Penny's room door was just slightly ajar. When did that happen? No one should have had access to that key. That thought totally flew out of my head as I flew through the air, crashing into the door after she pushed me—hard. I couldn't brace myself for the impact or for the next impact, which had my head smacking the bedpost at the foot of the bed.

I didn't pass out, thankfully, but I did lie there, stunned, as I heard the door slam shut and the key turn in the lock from the outside. Against my better judgment and the pounding in my head, I jumped to my feet and yanked my master key from the chain dangling from my waist.

It took less than a second to unlock the door and whip it open, but I didn't hear anything to show me where Sylvie had gone, until the painting at the top of the stairs fluttered open an inch before resettling itself.

How did she know about the back stairs? That didn't matter. What did matter was that she was going to enter the kitchen, where Glennis was cooking, and if I didn't get there soon enough, not only could Glennis be in trouble, but Sylvie could leave out of either door and never be seen again.

I had never hustled like I hustled down the front stairs. I could have followed her into the narrow staircase, but there was no guarantee that she wouldn't be waiting for me in those tight quarters.

Practically skipping down the stairs, I grabbed the newel post at the bottom to anchor me as I did a 180 to aim myself at the kitchen door. Aunt Hellen called out my name, but I had no time to stop and chat. Grabbing the door, I swung it open and then took in a scene that nearly made my heart stop.

Chapter 20

"Give me the code. I know you know the code, and you will tell me, or this knife doesn't stay idle."

Sylvie, that was Sylvie holding Glennis at knifepoint. And it wasn't just any knife, it was the biggest one from the butcher block on the prep table. She had it up against Glennis's neck and looked like she meant business.

They both looked at me as I entered the kitchen. I wanted to ram into Sylvie and knock the knife out of her hand, while also knocking her into the table, but that was far too risky. I had no way to ensure that Glennis wouldn't accidentally have that knife thrust into her throat.

Damn.

Holding up my hands to show Sylvie I had nothing in them, I let the door close behind me and waited for her next words.

Her eyes were watering. In rage? In sadness that she had been forced to this point for whatever reason that her mind had conjured up? I had no idea, but I did know that being the first to speak could make the threats become reality, and I didn't want that.

"What are you doing here?" Sylvie finally said. "You should go back the way you came in. I won't hurt this woman, as long as she gives me what I want. It's simple, really. I should have done this from the first day instead of waiting for a time when I had no other choice."

"I think we always have a choice," I said.

"Then you would be wrong." Sylvie scoffed. "So privileged, so able to do whatever you want, whenever you want. Do you know what it's like to be stuck in a family that you can't stand, but have no way out, unless you're willing to risk losing everything you've built?"

I couldn't say I did. But I did know about choices and about choosing to do the right thing for yourself when sometimes that felt like it would rock everyone around you.

Instead of answering, I just kept my eyes locked on her. Any second now, she was going to make a mistake, and I was going to have to be ready to launch myself at her when it was safe to do so. How had my life ended up like this?

"Well, it sucks. And when you finally have a chance to get things right, so you can leave, having someone thwart you is just one bridge too far. All I wanted was for Penny to give me the recipe card she stole from the kitchen."

Glennis stiffened up, and I willed her to stay absolutely still.

"Yeah, that recipe card. You have to know what you've been holding on to for the last thirty years, Glennis." She said Glennis's name with what could only be called a sneer.

"I don't, or rather I didn't."

"And now that you do, I need you to hand it over and give me the way to crack the code. I should have taken a picture of it when I first saw it, but I was so sure that Penny would understand that this could be the answer to all our issues. She could have her little affair with the guy who does her sleuthing, and I could leave her nephew, who is a jerk. It would have been a huge win for all of us. But no, she wanted to sit down for the one meal she'd allowed her nemesis to prepare for us, and she was going to out the whole story. It was important to her to have revenge. Me? Revenge is beneath me, but accidents do happen."

"Was killing Penny an accident then?" I asked, slowly inching toward the cabinet to my left. I highly doubted I'd be able to whip it open and grab a can of vegetables fast enough to wing it at her, but I didn't want to feel like I was doing nothing.

"Yes, of course it was. What a stupid question. Why would I want to kill my cash cow? She still had ties with the man's family she was supposed to marry into. All these years later, you would think she would have let things go, but not Penny. Despite having a full life after that botched betrothal thingy, she could never let it go. When I told her what the card was, she said she'd steal it, and she did. But then, she refused to give it to me. She was going to give it to the family because we weren't thieves."

"Wait a minute." Things were coalescing in my brain, and I needed clarification. "Are you saying that Penny was supposed to marry Anthony Fromm all those years ago?"

"Yes, she was. It was all mapped out. It wasn't a real betrothal though, like they hadn't had any formal paperwork. But it was what his family wanted, and he'd led her to believe that they'd get married one day. Then he met this one here, and all bets were off." She inched the knife toward Glennis's throat a little bit more. "He took off to make a different life. Penny was angry because it was supposed to be her, and then it wasn't. But she didn't know who it was instead. It wasn't until recently, when Anthony's dad finally died, that she decided to write that memoir. She said it was only because it had been thirty years, and she wanted to clear the slate before she keeled over. But I knew the truth, even if she wouldn't admit it until we got here. It was a cover so she could flesh out what had happened all those years ago."

"Let's back up a second." I would have been all too happy if she had chosen to take me literally and stepped away from Glennis, but from the glint in her eyes, that wasn't going to happen any time soon. "Penny was supposed to be married to this Anthony. He ducked out of her life, made a new one, and then what?" Because he certainly hadn't married Glennis. But according to Poobah, he'd told everyone that Anthony had died, or was that not the story she'd heard?

"Well, his family was told he'd drowned after being knocked off a ferry, but you have got to know that this part of the river never gets above five feet. They won't run the ferry if it's flooded. Why didn't he just stand up? He could have walked back to shore. Or why didn't anyone help him?"

I shook my head because I couldn't answer that one.

She kept right on going. "So, no, he didn't drown. He went on to hide out for the last thirty years, until his father died. He was supposed to testify against his dad for some shady dealings, but he decided after leaving here that he wasn't going to do it. His brother refused to be a part of whatever the family was up to, so the business died with his dad, and no one ever paid for anything they'd done wrong. The brother told us they came to an agreement that when the father died, Anthony had to hand over the recipe card because on the back is code for unlocking a safe that holds a ton of money and documents for the entire estate."

That was a lot for me to take in, but when I glanced over at Glennis, her eyes were void of anything. I would have expected her to cry or scream that Sylvie was wrong. Instead, she just stood there, like the robot Poobah had said she turned into when Anthony had supposedly died.

Yikes.

"I've seen the card," I said finally. I didn't tell her I had it on my phone because I was pretty sure that would only lead her to saying game over and pointing the knife at me. "There are no numbers on the back, it's all just a jumble of words that don't go together."

"That's true, but if you count up the value of each letter in each word according to where it lands on the alphabet, you get the combination."

"Wow, that's complicated." I wasn't sure what else to say, but it had gotten to the part of the story where I was afraid she was going to do something rash, and if I could keep her talking, there was every possibility Aunt Hellen was right outside the door, listening to our talk and hopefully coming up with a plan to get us out of here. Alive, preferably.

"Complicated can pay the bills and so much more, once I get my hands on that card. Now, tell me the code!" She jabbed forward a little and broke the skin on Glennis's neck, just a little bit, not a gusher, but we might not have long before that was her next action.

Think, Roxy, think!

"I have it on my phone," I said, even though I hadn't meant to. This was about Glennis's life, and I was willing to put everything on the table, let her run, and send Norm after her as soon as she left the premises if it meant no one was killed today. "I will give it to you, if you let Glennis go."

"I don't think I can do that now. We've gone too far. I was horrified at first when I hit Penny out of frustration and anger. I didn't mean to kill her, but then she slumped to the side, with blood running out of her temple, and I knew I couldn't undo it. Very *Clue* of me, I know. Ms. Penny, in the library with the candlestick. But what's done was done. And now I want to be finished with all this. And I will be, just as soon as you give me the card." She jabbed the knife again, and a bigger rivulet of blood seeped from Glennis's neck.

It was time to *do* something.

Taking a breath, I braced myself for impact and hoped against all hope that if I took Sylvie down by ramming her into the walk-in freezer door, made of steel, behind her that I could make sure that nothing more happened to Glennis.

And then the door swung open behind me, hitting me in the back and knocking me into her. We were both caught off guard, but I managed to bat the knife out of her hand as we hit the floor.

Norm stood above us for a split second with his [mouth] hanging open in shock, then snapped it shut and got to work.

Sylvie was cuffed as I helped Glennis up from the floor, where she had also fallen in our physical tussle.

"Are you okay?" I asked her over Sylvie's screaming fury at Norm and us and the world in general.

"So, he really is alive," she said, looking down at her hands braced on the prep table.

"It sounds that way." I stroked her back and waited to find out what she might tell me she needed.

"He'd contacted me, but I thought it was an imposter. That's where I was on the morning Penny died. I had arranged to meet up with whoever this person was and give them a piece of my mind, but they didn't show." She released a breath. "He called again, and I told him that I had nothing to say to him and to leave me alone. He asked for the recipe card for his family, and I told him he'd have to come and get it, knowing that he was dead, so there was no way anyone was going to show up." Wiping a hand over her face, she finally looked at me. "But he's real. And he really left me all those years ago, and your Poobah lied to me for all these years." She reached behind her below her waist, but nothing was there.

I ran around her and grabbed the stool from around the corner and then helped her settle into it. She had to be going through so much right now. Anger at Penny and Sylvie and their machinations was probably in there somewhere. Sadness for the life she never got to live. Maybe more anger at two men who had made decisions for her without her input. Shock that someone she'd loved over thirty years ago hadn't actually died, so all these years of mourning were actually for a lie.

Norm had Sylvie in cuffs and handed her over to Micah, who winked at me. Then Norm walked over to us and placed a hand on his aunt's shoulder. "I'm sorry, Aunt Glennis. I never really thought it was you. I would have figured it out eventually. Maybe I'm not as cut out for this as I thought I was."

That was quite the statement from the man who also thought he knew everything.

"Norm, you saved the day and caught the killer red-handed. Well, not actually with red on her hands, thanks goodness, because you got here right before she was going to do something very bad to Glennis." I reached forward and tipped her head to the side for Norm to see the puncture wounds.

"I'll take you to the hospital while they book her. Who knows what was on the knife?"

And for once, Glennis went along with something without having to be dragged into it.

I almost wished she had fought him because then at least I'd know she was still in there somewhere. Right now, she looked like a zombie, with little hope of ever coming out of that stasis.

As Glennis shuffled along behind him, Aunt Hellen gave them space to exit the kitchen, then immediately came in and shut the door. "I called emergency services as soon as I realized what was going on. I'm sorry they weren't here sooner. Is she okay?"

We both looked after Glennis and her nephew as she slowly trudged out the door, forgetting to close it behind her. Norm ran back and did it for her, sending us a worried look.

He was not alone on this one. I was worried, too, and wondering what came next.

Add it to my list, because when I looked up at the clock on the wall in the kitchen, I realized that dinner was in an hour, and I had no idea what the family was supposed to be eating. Not to mention that they would probably all know by then that one of their own was the killer of one of their own.

This called for lasagna.

Since I was not a great cook, that was all Glennis's territory, I put a call into the pizzeria down the street, and they were happy to accommodate me and add on some breadsticks.

I met them at the door, then carried all the food into the dining room. Clara and Taylor had set it up a few minutes ago, as I'd told them what had happened and asked if they'd be willing to fill in for Glennis if we were going to go through another shutdown for her. I had no doubt she'd try to do all the things, and I knew not to expect her to break, but having everyone on hand and high alert to help for the next little while was readily agreed to.

Everyone in the family trickled into the dining room with their immediate family, or by themselves if they weren't here with anyone else. I counted heads and got the correct number, which was now minus two.

Everyone took their seats, and it was obvious that they noticed that it was not a full table.

"Is Sylvie ever going to be on time, Michael? I tell you that girl has got a lot to answer for. I told her to be on her best behavior here. I cannot abide someone who is always only looking out for themselves!" Jessica said.

Funny, that coming from someone who very obviously also was often only out for themselves, from meals, to memoirs, to showing little to no sympathy for the people who might still be grieving the death of their mother and grandmother.

"Sylvie won't be joining you this evening," I said. Or for many evenings to come, I thought. "She's being questioned at the police station."

"What did she do now? Did she try to steal something from a museum? Or was she hiding away in that library, where she was supposedly studying? Personally, I think she was having an affair, but that's just me." Jessica glanced over at Leon, who flashed red, then she dropped her linen napkin into her lap, and it was all I could do not to knock her off her chair.

No wonder Sylvie had wanted to get out by any means possible. I wouldn't have made the choices she did, of course, but it might have been tempting if I thought it was the only way not to have to deal with this lousy bunch of people.

"Actually, it appears that she had something to do with Penny's death. They're questioning her now. Leon, you might also want to think about what parts you knew about this, since I saw her dive under your bed when I asked you to open the door for Sally."

I wasn't going to say anything more than that, even as the questions flew across the dining room table. I left through the door to the kitchen and then paused to watch them all fighting with each other. I didn't need the audio to know that things were heated when Sally shoved her chair back, pointing her finger at Leon, who refused to look at her. The rest of the table was either talking to each other or joining in the fight. Honestly, I didn't care what they were doing or saying. I only cared that they were all out of here first thing tomorrow morning.

"That's quite a ruckus out there," Poobah said as he joined me in the kitchen.

"It is. I'll be glad when they're gone, and I think we're only doing our family reunions here from now on. I can't take all this tension and angst."

"It's part of innkeeping." He plucked a strawberry from a bowl on the counter and bit into it. The color of the juice reminded me of the rivulet of blood that had rolled down Glennis's neck.

"You're going to want to brace yourself when Glennis returns. She knows that Anthony didn't die. I didn't say anything to her, before you jump to conclusions. Sylvie had the whole thing worked out and told her the story from her family's perspective and her research. Glennis shut down as soon as she told her that he had chosen to leave, but didn't die."

He sighed. "I knew this day would come at some point. I hoped it wouldn't, but I knew it would. I'll talk to her if she'll let me. If not then, I'm going to push harder this time instead of just allowing her to block everything out. It's what I should have done last time."

"I'm glad you feel that way." I turned to him and gave him a big hug. "I know you were trying to protect her, but she should have been given the truth and the ability to decide on her own what she'd do."

"You're absolutely right. And that's why I'm also here. I'm behind you a hundred percent on talking with Dean. Do it as soon as you can. We don't need the blessing from the conclave. They can't stop us from sharing our world with those we love. If they get testy, we'll just sic Mena on them and let her do her worst."

I chuckled into his chest, gave him a squeeze, and then let him go. "I think the toddler is about to start hurling bread at people. I should go in and see if they need anything."

"When you come back, I have a thought on the Ghost of Love thing. You didn't need it this time, but we still have to figure out what or who Amelia was able to contact by using the phone booth. Let's put our heads together tonight, and then we'll have a full week to think about it before we dive in."

I didn't necessarily want to wait a whole week until I could talk with Dean about Amelia's possible talents and see how his family thought about joining our family in tradition, but it made sense. I could be impulsive, but I'd waited this long, I could wait a little longer. If nothing else, I would have a week to build memories to cherish before Dean left me forever.

And I wouldn't even have a recipe card to hold onto.

That was a thought for another time.

Entering the dining room, I was surprised to find it tension-free and people talking in soft voices to each other.

"Everything okay in here?" I asked.

"Yes. Apparently, we have some stuff to work out, according to my son and Sally. We'll stay the night since it's already past the hour to check out, if that's okay with you. We'll be gone first thing in the morning. I don't know that we'll ever come back, but that's not due to your hospitality or the wonderful staff you have on hand. We'll highly recommend you and your inn to anyone who asks. I'm sorry it turned out this way." Jessica. That was Jessica talking to me in a conciliatory tone that took me off guard.

It appeared to take everyone else off guard, too, and the volume escalated, but not with anger this time. I let myself out of the dining room, leaving them to do whatever talking they needed to do in order to deal with this new reality.

And I backed right into Dean.

"Oh, sorry!" I said, smiling up at him. I raised my chin to get a quick kiss, but he held onto my elbow, then stepped back, and dropped his gaze to the floor.

What was this? Please don't make me have to say goodbye right as I was planning on making things right. Please!

He cupped the back of his neck with one of his strong hands, rocking back on his heels.

"Whatever it is you have to say, just say it. The dread is pretty high right now, so your words aren't going to make it worse. I'd rather know whatever truth you have to tell me than you leaving and never saying goodbye."

"Goodbye?"

"What else would make you look like this?" My stomach hurt, but whatever happened, I would make it through. I had a strong family, a strong inn, and a heart that had survived until now without a partner. I'd figure out how to do it again.

He blew out a sigh. "Okay, look, it's about my family. I can't keep things from you when I know that I want to make a life with you. Marry you. You might not be ready for that just yet, or maybe this week is like a trial run, but I can't keep quiet knowing what I know and not telling you."

What on earth was he talking about?

I didn't respond fast enough. He walked away, but then he turned back around and came right back.

"It's about Amelia."

"Okay..."

"She can...do things. I don't know how to explain it, and in fact, I don't know that I'm allowed to explain it, but I can't keep this a secret from you and expect you to want to be with me. I need honesty. I didn't have it for a long time. Heck, even my last name isn't my real last name, but with you, I want to be honest. I want you to know my bad, my good, my..."

"Magic?"

That got him to stare straight into my eyes. He searched there for something, and I hoped he found it. If not, I'd show him.

"Magic, yes."

"I've watched her make swirls in the river when she feels like she might get in trouble. The wind kicks up when she's in a mood, and the sky can go completely dark if she's angry. It doesn't last long, but when I consulted my books and looked at the previous talents that have run down through the ages, I'm thinking she's an aeromancer. I'll have to consult the guide Poobah has to make sure, but I'm pretty confident that's her talent. Has she had any training?"

To say he looked like his gob had been smacked, or his flabber had been gasted, would have been an understatement.

"You know?"

"I don't know everything, but I do know some things. And that humming you thought I was doing was a book talking to me. I'm a bibliomancer. I talk to books, and they talk back." My hands felt itchy, and sweat was rolling down my back, but this had to be done.

"Well, I'll be damned."

"Or blessed. I guess it depends on how you look at it."

He laughed and grabbed me up in a hug. "You have no idea how much I've been dreading this."

"Oh, I think I might."

He squeezed me harder and then set me back on my feet.

"I'm sure this is totally the wrong time to ask, and I don't have all the things with me that I need, but that marrying thing was something I'm very serious about. If it's too early for you..."

I cut him off with a kiss as I twined our hands together, like handfasting. Another adventure. One I desperately wanted to explore with my very own Watson.

I drew my head back a little after a minute. "Where's my ring?" I asked.

"That's somewhere on my list for this week during our stay-cation."

"Let's move it up to priority number one."

"Done."

And it was. Now to tell the rest of the family and hope that we were no longer in the sleuthing business. I had other plans for my Watson that did not include taking time away from building us.

GET THE LAST BOOK IN THE SERIES!

Misty Simon, who also writes as Gabby Allan, always wanted to be a storyteller. Today, she has more than 30 titles to date in the romance and mystery genres. She lives with her husband in Central Pennsylvania where she is hard at work on her next novel or three. www.mistysimon.wordpress.com